The world is all that is the case.

LW

Other books by Marc Estrin

Fiction

*Proceedings of The Hebrew Free Burial Society for Indigent Jews
on Staten Island*
The Penseés of Alan Krieger by Alan Krieger
Kafka's Roach: the Life and Times of Gregor Samsa
Hyde
Speckled Vanities
And Kings Shall Be Thy Nursing Fathers
The Prison Notebooks of Alan Krieger (Terrorist)
When the Gods Come Home to Roost
Tsim-tsum
The Good Doctor Guillotin
The Annotated Nose
Skulk
The Lamentations of Julius Marantz
Golem Song
The Education of Arnold Hitler
Insect Dreams, the Half Life of Gregor Samsa

Translations

*Whatever Befalls: Johannes Hösle: Poems from the Dietenbronn
Neurological Clinic*
*Notes of Devastation: A Compilation and Singing Translation
of Heinrich Schütz's Three Passion Settings*

Memoirs

The Insect Dialogues (with Fred Ramey)
*Rehearsing With Gods: Photographs and Essays on the Bread
& Puppet Theater* (with Ron Simon, photographer)

Et Resurrexit

Marc Estrin

Fomite
Burlington, VT

ISBN-13: 978-1-959984-40-5
Library of Congress Control Number: 2023950865

Fomite
58 Peru Street
Burlington, VT 05401
www.fomitepress.com
11-22-2023

PROLOGUE

TAPHOPHOBIA

From G. ταφοσ (*taphos*) (grave) + phobia: the fear of being buried alive.

The above drop cap is the only one to be used in this book. It has dropped, SLAM. The top covers you, CLANG, and there are you below, lying not parallel to it, but perpendicular to it, as in the T, pushing up against it, trying to lift it again; beating your pathetic fist against it, hoping someone will hear, become curious, and come to your rescue.

Probably not.

And yet it must have happened, or how can we account for the plethora of in-grave signaling devices invented and paid for in case of premature burial? Someone, somewhere, sometime in the days before general embalming and the growth of mortuary sophistication, must have demonstrated the need. Something must have happened and made the headlines. A deep coma, or state of "suspended animation" might have landed someone in one hell of a mess. But fear and engineering to the rescue:

One of the first heroic patents (1843), useful only pre-burial, was for a spring-loaded coffin lid, triggered by the slightest movement of head or hand. Another, designed in 1868 for potential use post-burial, provided a ladder within a cylinder leading above ground, and, if the corpse was too weak to climb, a bell to signal. Several patent-years later, there was a chain which, with a slight pull, would allow air into the coffin space while electromagnetically ringing an attention-getting bell, and loosing a spring-loaded red flag to signal a wish for disinterment. Lest you think of these as being quaintly and comically pre-modern, in 2021, because it represented a potentially significant theo-scientific experiment, the Hebrew Free Burial Society for Indigent Jews allowed to be installed in the fresh coffin of one Alan N. Krieger: "an array of intra-coffin electrical, chemical and acoustical sensors connected to an alarm system at the HFBSFIJ office; an EEG 12-lead Monitor, EEG-Pro/Dragon Dictate software, and an above-ground solar Powerwall™ to drive the experimental equipment in perpetuity, together with the initial findings from that array all generously donated by Elon Musk." And Elon Musk is no dummy. Human torpor, natural, or artificially induced, remains a possibility even today, and certainly back in the drug-soaked sixties . But forewarned is not necessarily forearmed.

Somebody, sometime, somewhere, must have escaped from the tomb.

PART ONE

On Wednesday, Apr 13, 1968, at approximately 5:30 PM, the Vanderbilt-Davidoffs, at their late afternoon cocktails, were surprised to see a greasy auto-hauler with out-of-state plates roll up the driveway, and park in front of their elegant Westchester home. Strapped down in the rear was not a car, but a cardboard box resembling nothing so much as a casket. They hadn't ordered any large appliances.

And on that same Wednesday, Apr 13, 1968, at approximately 7:30 PM, William Eugene Vanderbilt-Davidoff rose from the dead.

In leaving the casket, he demonstrated that undertakers, or at least the under-undertakers and mini-morticians at Mt. Kisco's Dignity Funeral Home and Services, spent as little time with their deceased as one might expect. After all, they might reason, who is there to talk to, and about what?

Upon discovering Mr. Vanderbilt-Davidoff's open, empty casket, and after a short staff meeting, Randy, Jim, and Lamont decided to replace Will with four bags of roadway salt laid end to end, and to close the coffin. Screw it down. It was a closed-casket contract. Who would know? And Dignity FH&S could hardly afford the scandal of having lost a client.

What were some of their theories?

Randy thought perhaps he was not really dead.

"Trying to pull off some hoax. Disappear from the law."

"What do you suppose he did?"

"Who knows?"

"Where'd we pick him up?"

"We didn't. His parents and some tow truck brought him in"

Jim supposed someone might have stolen his body.

Maybe he was killed for ransom or something."

"Or like maybe they want to give him to a medical school or something."

"Med schools don't need more bodies."

"Maybe for something like a Frankenstein experiment."

Lamont reasoned that he was maybe only half-dead.

"It's possible. Not entirely plausible, but possible."

"Supernatural."

Randy: "Everything isn't always natural. Laws of nature are statistical, and this could be far out on the probability curve. We might have to revisit the idea of what we mean by possible or impossible."

"What if he had something he really needed to do?"

"Like what?"

"I dunno. Turn off the burner on some stove. Feed a cat."

"Sweatshirt says St. John's College. Didn't he rise from the dead or something?"

What none of them considered was that Will had come by his astonishing savoir-vivre-savoir-morir honestly, and not without significant sacrifice. And this was his culminating *coup de theatre*.

HIS PARENTAGE

William Eugene Vanderbilt-Davidoff was the blessed product of an interfaith coupling featuring a one-God egg with a one-Pope sperm, a marriage illegal and cursed by both sets of in-laws, a classic of star-crossed lover dalliance.

Why was he named Will? Was it Grandfather Cyrus's insistence that infant Eugene (Gr. well-born) take his son's, Will's father's, name? There is a peculiarity among some Catholic families — perhaps due only to weakness of imagination or intellect—which favors naming a first son after the father. But no, Cyrus Vanderbilt had very little to say about it. He had been dead for two decades.

Was it after William Shakespeare? William Wordsworth? Will Rogers? Will Durant? None of the above.

In fact his overly-brainy parents, Charles

and Gwen, had named him after Schopenhauer's masterwork, *The World as Will and Representation,* of which they were sharing a copy at the time. Hey, why not? He'd always have a conversation starter for cocktail parties, or to impress coedish girlfriends. The name could pass for normal under normal-demanding circumstances, and since his two parents had cumulatively four names, so should he, their combination and multiplication: William Eugene Vanderbilt-Davidoff. And his ensuing initials would be a free recursive nod to their favorite multilingual radio station, WEVD, its call letters subversively celebrating Eugene V. Debs, a half-century dead, but not forgotten by either end of the ancestral spectrum. Yes, *that* Eugene V. Debs, socialist, activist, unionist, founding member of the IWW, and five times candidate for president, whose main message was to blame capitalism for war.

Gwen's delicatessen family, the Davidoffs, had voted for Debs in 1912, an election in which he — running as a socialist — won 6% of the vote. They

voted for him again in 1916, and again in 1920, a
campaign famously run from his prison cell, Debs a
victim of Woodrow Wilson's 1917 anti-sedition law,
the Espionage Act, upheld by the Supreme Court
in 1919, whose ghost haunts American politics even
now.

Even Charlie's Family scrapbook contained a
clipping which read

> William H. Vanderbilt
> [Charlie's great-great]
> by Eugene V. Debs
> editorial snippet in
> Locomotive Firemen's
> Magazine, vol. 10, no. 3
> (March 1886)
>
> William H. Vanderbilt,
> before his death, gave one
> of his boys a million dollars.
> His grandfather [Cornelius
> Vanderbilt] gave him a
> million, and now the young

> man starts in business with
> $2 million. If he attends
> strictly to business, waters
> his stock, sands his sugar,
> etc., he may manage to
> make a living. If he should
> fail, however, his father
> can set him up again. If a
> Locomotive Fireman could
> work 4,444 years, 300 days
> each year, at $1.50 per day,
> he would be in a position
> to bet Mr. Vanderbilt $2.50
> that all men are born equal.

During McCarthy's reign, Charlie remembered his family discussing "the poison of disloyalty", and chuckling all around.

And so — Debs not withstanding — Will it would be. Will. As in *The World as Will and Representation*. Not William, and never to be Bill or Billy. But the Schopenhauer link would be no joke, though as joke it started out.

Will's first tux was a sleeper bag from Bergdorf-
Goodman's, with a Superman S insignia woven into
the front. And why not? Though pentagon it may be,
it was cute. Besides, both philosophy-major parents
realized the S could, should, and probably would,
stand for more than Superman. Socrates, perhaps,
or Schopenhauer. Will looked more like some
misplaced old man, than any mere new-born should.
Then again, he was handsome even, if you squinted.
Sinatra, maybe, the crooner, though only new parents
could love his songs. S for sinister? S for SHAZAM?
This they hadn't even thought of, and did not know.

Who were the parents that deliberating such names?
Vanderbilt-Davidoff. Let's begin with the more
obvious.

CHARLES

Charles Peterson Vanderbilt (b. 1940) was the
great-great-great-great (I think four greats and a

grand is correct) grandson of Cornelius Vanderbilt, the eminent shipping and railroad magnate of the Gilded Age, scion of the once-wealthiest family in the United States, a man who had made his money by out-foxing Robert Fulton. Whose company, at the time, had a monopoly on all mercantile traffic into and out of New York harbor. But the "Commodore", whose fleet was based in New Jersey, nevertheless steamed his little navy of trade vessels in and out of the harbor, flying a flag that read "NEW JERSEY MUST BE FREE!" His lawyer, Daniel Webster, successfully argued the case before the US Supreme Court, leaving behind one of the first laws concerning the freedom of interstate commerce: freedom to make a killing.

That killing enabled Charlie Peterson Vanderbilt to go to Eton College, the largest boarding school in England, home to sons of world leaders, and of world-famous stars of stage and screen. His summary of the school: "It doesn't matter how idiotic you are, as long as you're rich. Foreign, stupid, criminal, no matter. All that matters is that you can pay." As you might imagine, our Will's father was not very good at being rich...

...as was obvious from his pre-post-partum purchase of a Westchester County home. Towards the end of his wife's pregnancy, Charlie had laid out, in cold cash, three million dollars for an English-style country home on five acres in Mt. Kisco. His burgeoning, now-almost-three-person family demanded no less.

Most rich people do not pay large amounts of cash for planes, or yachts or homes, because they can invest their money more profitably elsewhere instead of putting out some large sum. Not Charlie. Sight unseen, from an ad in a real estate flyer, he had purchased an "upscale", though tasteful-looking mansion with custom-crafted inlaid floors. No shoes in this house. There was a billiard room downstairs (off limits to children) and a two-story library, which would provide engagement and fun for four-year old Will, running the ladder around its track. Will's was the home-and-school wing upstairs — his parents slept in a private wing downstairs in their large, custom, antique,

European four-poster bed, no jumping allowed. I
leave the home theater (35mm) and the swimming
pool (oversize) to your imagination. Young Will was
embarrassed to bring friends home.

GWEN

His mom, on the other hand, grew up poor, the
daughter of a delicatessen, even though with
one spectacular, world-famous relative way back:
Ignaz Semmelweis. Ignaz the Despised, Ignaz
the Disdained, Ignaz the Dope. These were the
nicknames he had earned for being right. Finally
known as "the savior of mothers", Dr. Semmelweis
had discovered that the incidence of childbed fever,
often fatal, could be drastically reduced if physicians
would only wash their hands before assisting
at births. You can imagine the " What-do-you-
think-we-are, dirty-pigs?" defenses put up, and the
counter-accusations against a Hungarian immigrant,
pre-germ-theory upstart. In fact, his colleagues had
him committed to a mental asylum, where, trying to

escape, he was worked over by guards, and died two weeks later from a gangrenous hand wound, inflicted at the beating. Wash your hands, indeed!

No good deed goes unpunished — by infection if necessary. Semmelweis's story is not an encouraging one for those with faith in medical professionals.

No more encouraging, five generations later, was the story of the Vanderbilts' reaction to Charlie's bringing home a "Jewess". A Jewess whose father and mother ran a delicatessen? Why not someone "of quality"? The least she could do would be to change her name to Davis or Donaldson. What would the wedding announcement in the *Times* look like — a Vanderbilt groom taking a Davidoff bride? They would pay her $3,000 to have her name officially changed. She was reluctant. Her parents, she said, would be embarrassed, upset. Embarrassed at her marrying into economic royalty? What kind of a crazy woman was their son taking on? $5,000? Six? Charlie won her heart and mind with his defense of her, and his insistence.

At 18, Gwen had gone off to NYU on full

scholarship, the first in the family to attend college. And from there, like Charlie, to Cornell, just after the war. Though both in Ithaca (not the homeland of Odysseus, the other one), they had brought with them vastly different baggage.

Gwen's was, in fact, a Penelope-like patience, and a lurking disdain for her several lower-class, if mostly lefty, suitors. Charlie, at first, did not inspire. Though not a seriously-Jewish, lower-east-side Jewish girl, a thin patina of Jewishness had here and there put down tap roots in Gwen's psyche.

The Orthodox Judaism all around her did not at all sanction the validity or even legitimacy of intermarriage. That attitude, she sensed, was not correct, and might even be part cause of the antisemitism toward "the Jews — who had gotten us into the war." She felt repulsed by that sense of superiority and chosenness. "Goys" "not good enough to marry us"? Goys polluting our Jewish blood, distancing us from God — though after the war and the discovery of the camps, who except the Orthodox really believed in God?

Even the Conservative Jews she had met at NYU, while being OK with a non-Jewish spouse, would hope for his or her conversion, and would want the children of such a marriage to be circumcised and "raised Jewish". While with the postwar Reform Jews, there was little Judaism left to reform. Whatever they felt like calling "Jewish", was Jewish. But a chosen germ plasm remained.

Plus, there had been Mannie — Emmanuel Bronner.

This chemistry/philosophy major had come to the US in 1923, when Gwen was six, leaving his parents behind to the as-yet-unimagined Holocaust. At Cornell in 1946, having heard some of the gruesome details of his parents' fate, he decided to become a soap-maker, but of GOOD soap, replete with, and wrapped in, good ideas, printed in dark sky-blue.

His name, Emmanuel, meant "God with us" in Hebrew. It was the name given to Christ by Isaiah — Christ, the deliverer of Judah. He would share his philosophy through soap, and his texts would be studied as people washed themselves clean in bathtubs around the world.

SOAP in medicine is the mnemonic for writing up patient visits — Subjective, Objective, Assessment, and Plan. And Emmanuel Bronner's soap, would encompass all that in its prescriptions. "We must realize our transcendent unity across religious and ethnic divides or perish." Not on your average soap label. He had a peace plan to "unite the spaceship, where we unite all mankind...All-One or None! All-One!"

Bronner's prescriptions: "We're all sisters & brothers! You & I, Here & Now, Today! Not them nor they! You & I Today! 1st: If I'm not for me, who am I? Nobody! 2nd: Yet if I'm only for me, what am I? Nothing! 3rd: If not now, when???!!! Unite we must!"

That's a lot of exclamation points. Imagine going on a date with this guy.

One date was enough, and though not specifically Jewish, his ravings seemed to Gwen to embody all the moral over-earnestness and mental hyperactivity of the street speaker crazies on Union

Square, Jewish anarchists and communists, fiercely intent on saving the world.

Leaving the city for Cornell, she wanted more air to breathe.

But while you can take the Jew out of Jewishness, you can't take Jewishness out of the Jew. It came with her to Ithaca.

And even deeper for Gwen than her Jewishness were her habits of poverty. Later in life, though living in a three million dollar home, with 18 rooms and three servants, she still clipped coupons, and if she had ever to shop, would carry them with her, alphabetized, in her "shmata bag". Young Will was too ashamed to accompany her in any cash register line. "I'll meet you at the car — which was always waiting close outside, chauffeur at the wheel. "My meshugeneh Mama," he would have said, if he could bear the sound or idea of speaking Yiddish.

A major in South Asian Studies, during her Cornell Junior Year Abroad, Gwen saw enough poverty in her semester in India to make her an anti-imperialist, and also enough to make her want to be rich, rich, rich. Charlie's timid wooing became suddenly more attractive.

WOOING

That wooing had begun at Norman Malcolm's Wittgenstein Summer Seminar. During an extraordinarily hot July summer of '49, the great man himself attended a handful of graduate philosophy seminars there. A small, odd-looking person, most intense, shabbily dressed, and using a cane, he would walk into a classroom and simply stand there, awaiting a question. Gwen had courageously asked him if he thought "ought", as in "ought to", necessarily implies "can" — possibility of so doing. He spent a minute or two looking out the window, as class members sat breathless awaiting an answer. Then, he turned slowly around and snapped, "I refuse to stand here and discuss stupid questions."

After he left the room, the group spent much time exploring the meaning and implications of his remark. Charlie alone thought him rude, and

disrespectful of his student hosts, defending the
legitimacy, and even depth, of Gwen's question.
That was how their summer affair had begun, and
persisted into the fall, and into their marriage...

...AND AHEAD TO CHILD WILL

In April of 1950, in a sterile operating room
at Presbyterian (Presbyterian!) Hospital that
Semmelweis would have extolled, Gwen Davidoff
was safely, antiseptically, delivered of a premature
baby boy. Outside, in the waiting room, sat Morris
and Ida Davidoff, they of Davidoff's Deli, Eighth St.
and Second Ave, and across from them, taciturn, at
maximum distance, were Cornelius Vanderbilt Jr. and
his wife, Anna, neé Needham, 25 years younger, once
his secretary — Charlie's Mum and Dad.

Infant Will's first cognomen had been Childe
Fatso, for he was a chubby one. Seven days later,
came his first family crisis: the question of whether
to go ahead with circumcision.

The Vanderbilts would have been against it

because, well, you know, Jews. Plus traditional Christian *caritas*, even though sometimes manifesting as burning at the stake, though in this case expressed as "Why cause the child unnecessary pain?"

The Davidoffs would have been for it because, well, you know, Jews, even though the practice had sometimes resulted in "Drop your pants!", broken glass, free transport, and worse.

In the early 50's the universal Socrates of baby and childcare was Benjamin Spock. Benjamin? Jewish? But was Ben Franklin Jewish? Spock? Who knows? It wasn't Smith, but it wasn't Spiegelman. The trouble was that Dr. Spock himself was of two minds.

In the forties and fifties, Spock had preached circumcision performed within a few days of birth, since such a practice would have no chance of "scaring the bejeebers" out of a young boy. But more recently, as Freud's ghost swept over and into the mid-century American mind, Dr. Spock began to reconsider the issue, and, while not yet changing the text of his bible, had privately admitted to friends that "If I had the good fortune to have another son, my choice would be to leave his little penis alone."

How did the public know this? They didn't. But the Vanderbilts were not the public. They had friends in high places, places as high as the upper reaches of NY Presbyterian Hospital, and the top floor where the elite of the medical elite sipped their coffees to stay awake for the upcoming heart surgeries, and discussed the latest trends — like *asking* parents about circumcision, and not just assuming it. The Vanderbilt family doctor was married to the head of Pediatrics, a friend of Dr. Spock's, and by the normal process of percolation and filtration, the notion of choice had reached young Charles, long before *Baby and Childcare* changed its tune in the 80s.

So — she, FOR, though she didn't really know why; he, AGAINST, for reasons only rumored. To tell the truth, I don't really know the outcome, since I had never asked. Either way, Will was probably unremarkable in the Fieldstone Upper shower room.

The success of the parental marriage was not

so guaranteed. The happy future of their union,
Cornell-imbued, Wittgenstein-catalyzed, financially
over any conceivable top, might have been
considered a no-brainer by the uninformed, but
not quite a marriage made in heaven, and equally
not a marriage made in hell. Given their mixed
backgrounds, it was more like a marriage made in
Sheol, a condition not so thoroughly explored.

Hell is pretty easy, from Joyce's definitive sermon
in *Portrait*, to Sartre's "Hell is other people", to Gary
Larson's hilarious, hell-obsessed cartoons — the
range has been covered. What it's really like depends
on the inmate.

Heaven, blinding at best, boring at worst, has
been less successfully imagined and described, even
by Dante. The rose of divine love, angels flitting
around it like bees, the wheels within wheels, how a
Buddhist would laugh! Or a Jew think "Oi, veh!"

But Sheol, now there's a challenge. In the
Hebrew bible, which neither Charles nor Gwen
could read — though for them it might be
required reading — Sheol is the gray waiting space,

"the abode of the dead", "the common grave of
mankind", where, after death, all must go — to
sleep in a region dark and deep, "oblivion". It is not
the Hades of Greek mythology, nor the Hell of
Christian imagination. There is no gloomy Satan on
his throne, or his minions, patrolling and poking.
The sleepers, post-Jesus, await the resurrection
of the body, purified, perhaps, in a fiery furnace.
What a marriage counselor would do with this is
anybody's guess.

Aside from newborn-related loss of sleep and its
accompanying irritability, the first real family crisis
came in late August, 1949, a crisis of which 5-month
old Will was completely unaware.

Paul Robeson in Peekskill

Charlie Vanderbilt was long an aficionado of vocal
art. His family box at the Met had brought him tens,
if not a hundred hearings of the great operatic voices
of the forties and fifties. Yes, he had missed Caruso.

But Pavarotti, Marian Anderson, Maria Callas, Andrea Bocelli, Jan Peerce, Eileen Farrell, Jesse Norman, Mario Lanza, Joan Sutherland, Ezio Pinza, José Carreras, Kirsten Flagstad ... he had heard them all. But even after all of them, the voice that had most struck him was not at the Met at all, but in a film he had seen at Cornell, several years before Will had been born, the 1936 James Whale production of Hammerstein and Kern's *Showboat*.

Ol' Man River, dat ol' man river, he jus keep rollin', he mus' know somepin, he jus keep rollin' along, he sang to himself as he drove the Packard up the Saw Mill River Parkway towards Peekskill. But try as he might, and no matter how he pressed his chin to his chest, he could not come up with Paul Robeson's rich basso profundo, so easily recalled by his acoustic brain. When he heard Robeson would be singing, a few hours drive from the city, he determined to go, in spite of the violence of the previous week's concert in the same area. Surely the police had been alerted to the danger, and the concert would be adequately protected.

Well, yes, the police were alerted, but a significant number of them were on the side of their friends and neighbors in resisting foreign invasion. Should they try coming again, local patriots were ready to receive the Commie, nigger-loving Jews that had invaded their quiet community to listen to an uppity black man sing about Russia, and civil rights, and looking for trouble. They had had a week to gather rocks, and pile them along the narrow dirt road which would be become the only permitted exit from the Lakeland Acres picnic area — an open lawn which faced a military cemetery for those who had "paid the supreme price to insure our democratic government."

Approaching Peekskill, there were men and women lining the side of the road, shaking their fists and screaming at him to go home, and in the center of town, an American Legion Band, parading "The Stars and Stripes Forever", in protest of the Robeson concert. Hurrah for the flag of the free! Jew! Commie bastard! Kike! Nigger-lover! Red!

The Cortlandt Manor concert had gone well enough, in spite of, or perhaps because of, the police helicopter throbbing overhead. There was tension in the air, but the unions, the Communist Party, and groups of Robeson's followers had arranged a security circle, linked hand in hand around the entire circumference. 20,000 people heard Pete Seeger lead the crowd in "*If I Had a Hammer*", and Robeson sing some Russian folksong, "*Go Down, Moses*", the final aria from Boris Godunov ("*Fight with me to free the land of our fathers!*"), and seven other songs — Negro spirituals, "*America the Beautiful*", closing with "*Ol' Man River*".

The first hint of trouble came when the Peekskill police funneled the exit traffic not the way people had entered, but into a winding, narrow dirt road through the surrounding woods, which turned out to be lined with a mile-long gauntlet of veterans and their families, with rocks stacked along the way in size place, beginning with the fist-size smallest. Charles was glad he hadn't brought the Bentley.

But the Packard was solid. The first rock caused only a spidery crack in the right side window, but the second, following hard upon, opened up the glass with a one inch wound. Charley had been warned by several of his concert-mates to keep windows rolled up on the way out, though it would be a typically warm, early-September afternoon. What the well-wishers didn't know was that any car having its windows rolled up was seen as an enemy vehicle, and a reasonable target: only the Robeson crowd would have their windows up. Neighbors, even if for some reason they wanted to hear Robeson, would certainly have their windows down, with their elbows propped up on the frames.

The exit was gruelingly slow, with cars, trucks, and buses moving stop and go, bumper to bumper, no faster than a man could walk. Once in line, there was no turning around, no way out, no way back. Two cars ahead of Charles's, a door was pulled open, and two Negroes pulled out — to the tune of "Kill the niggers! Kill 'em!" A nearby state cop sidled up to the attackers, and encouraged them to put their haul back into the car: they were holding up traffic. When one of the beaten men rose up too slowly from the ground, he was aided by an energetic kick in the groin as the trooper nodded, and looked approvingly on. Charles thought it better not to intervene, as he, too, would be holding up traffic. Driving home, what rolled unmercifully, over and over through his head, were the last lines Robeson had sung

> *I gits weary and sick of tryin'*
> *I'm tired of livin' and scared of dyin'*
> *But Ol' Man Ribber, dat Ol' Man Ribber,*
> *He jus' keep rollin' along.*

Why end with that, Charles wondered, when Robeson's life was so courageously dedicated otherwise? Did he know something Charlie didn't?

Governor Thomas E. Dewey blamed communists for provoking the violence. Other cities became fearful of similar incidents, and over 80 scheduled Robeson concert dates of were canceled. He would be blacklisted, his passport revoked, and with the CIA and MI5 on his case, succumb to a well-earned paranoia.

When, returning home early that evening,

Gwen asked him how the concert was, all he could say before dropping to bed fully-clothed was, "Fine. Good." Of all this, Will knew nothing. The Packard knew quite a lot.

First Conundrum

The crisis of which Will was quite aware came a few months later, is lightly called "toilet training", and more accurately, "sphincter control", though that is the term of the conqueror, not the vanquished. Custom-crafted inlaid floors are not for peeing and pooping on, in spite of the downstairs maid's ability to competently clean them up with no apparent rancor. Even less for peeing and pooping on are eighteenth and nineteenth century Persian, Turkish, and Iranian rugs, barely worn out, and if worn out at all, worn out by the socked feet of kings and princesses, and not so easily cleaned without sending them out. Will's first mistake was his last. Fortunately it was a well-formed specimen, and though never having owned a dog, daddy Charles was aware of the expression "rub his nose in it". So, gripping him tightly by the back of the neck, he forced Will's nose quite close to his leavings, but not so close so as to have to also clean his face.

The whole business was a bit confusing to Will, since, in fact, he liked the je ne sais quoi smell, and he couldn't tell if the paternal gesture was one of punishment or treat. It might very well have been the latter, since it was concluded by a fine paternal swing and carry to one of the downstairs bathrooms, "his" bathroom, where a kingly potty seat and changing table had been installed.

Enter, once again, (as always with Will) Dr. Benjamin Spock. *Baby and Child Care*, still claimed pride of place in the Master Bedroom. Even that 6'4" peacenik famously warned that there was "no way out of that power struggle", except to ease off on it. He warned that strict, i.e. punishable, training could lead to behavioral problems, as wartime anthropologists studying Japanese soldiers had also concluded. It was the toddler him or herself that would invite this new curriculum into his or her life. The 1946 edition of "Spock", as the Vanderbilts called this bible, instructed parents to "leave bowel training almost entirely up to your baby.... [who] will probably take himself to the toilet before he is two years old."

Note the "probably". And what if not? Will was quickly approaching two. He had a decision to make: poop-filled diapers, or freedom. Along the way, and while being exposed to, instructed in, the wonders of modern American upper-class plumbing, he was torn. Mum and Dad seemed to be patiently awaiting his second birthday, while he continued trying to outwit the safety pins without being able to unpin them. His hips were slim enough that with some Houdini-like exertions, he could often slip the diaps to the floor, step free, and poop or pee without "soiling himself", as one of the maids delicately put it - the one who was assigned to cleanup. So, finally, as the good doctor had noted, it was his choice.

But he would have had to admit that the toilet

itself, the seat with the ducky splash cup, the seat that was placed, throne-like, up on the regular toilet seat, his other high chair, were all structurally, architecturally impressive. More impressive still, was the swirling down of his poops, the de-yellowing of the toilet water, as disposal proceeded. Where did it go? Down. Down where? Down into the pipes. What pipes? The pipes under the house. Where did the pipes take it? ... I don't know (nobody did). Somewhere.

He would grip the porcelain bowl in fear and wonder as he watch his leavings going down somewhere deep, into the bowels of the earth (what a strange expression!) (Origin: Middle English: from Old French *bouel*, from the Latin *botellus*, diminutive of *botulus*, 'sausage'. How even stranger!) And the vortex. As Poe would have it, the "Descent into the Maelstrom." It became an ongoing leitmotif —
descent, and determined resurrection.

There were three cameras in the Vanderbilt household: a top-or-the-line Paillard Bolex 5340

16mm cine film camera with a full complement
of lenses, lens filters, hoods and caps. It was
occasionally used to shoot outdoor events, but rarely
were the films projected or seen again.

Far more utilized were the family's two still
cameras — Gwen's Kodamatic bellows camera,
and Charlie's Leica M11 Rangefinder. The first
took snapshots, the second, photographs. The
first required pointing and clicking, the second,
artistic considerations of lighting, focus, grayscale
and framing. At one point or another, both had
been focused on Will on the toilet, producing
images sure to embarrass any teenager flipping
through the family album to loosen up a potential
girlfriend.

THE DEEPER CONUNDRUM

Was Will's fascination with poops' underground fate,
and the refilling of cleansed toilet water enough to
explain his future antics? No. The core issues were
musical. Not that the flushing and refilling of a toilet

doesn't supply music of its own, but that particular concert is more metaphorical than actual, even if John Cage might try to notate and perform it. I'm talking about what the outside world might actually consider as songs, and the traumatic path they created. Four songs and three concerts had lit Will's way into darkness.

The earliest began in the first row balcony of the New York City Center. On the night in question, the New York City Ballet was performing Balanchine's new choreography for Stravinsky's *Firebird*, starring Maria Tallchief, with scenery and costumes by Marc Chagall. In a feverishly anticommunist atmosphere, presenting Russian music at all risked maniacal attack, but Firebirds had no discernible politics. What they did have was an evil sorcerer controlling them, Koschei the Deathless, his vulnerable soul hidden inside nested objects, places and conditions. What happened in the ballet Will did not remember. What he did remember was Koshei the Deathless.

Deathlessness is a haunting idea for a six-year

old just beginning to understand his parents', and worse, his own, mortality. The fact that Koschei the Deathless seemed pretty dead at the end only made things more confusing. Parents should be careful about what they subject their children to in the name of culture.

For instance, a rich kid's "European Heritage Tour" in the fall of that same Koschei year only kneaded the deathy dough. Charles Vanderbilt's father's ancestors, as far as one could tell, came from the town of DeBilt, east of Utrecht, in the Netherlands. And there, their tour began. As was their usual touring practice, they would conclude a long day of sight-seeing with dinner in the town's finest restaurant, attending a concert or play, or whatever main event was on the calendar, and an overnight at a pre-booked suite in the best hotel. In De Bilt that night they happened to land on a performance of the B-minor Mass at the Immanuelkerk De Bilt. What luck! (Little did they know.) Who could turn that down? But turn it down, they should have. For before falling asleep, their tired six-year old, fell into and down another vortex — the space between life and death.

Like most modern, and especially mixed-family, kids, Will knew little about either of his parents' ancestral religions. And as with most six-year olds, the most, indeed only, interesting parts (the crucifixion, the crusades, the concentration camps) had to do with violence and killing. For all the musical genius, the b-minor Mass can't be very interesting to a sleepy kid raised on American musical comedy. It starts in Greek, and goes into Latin, neither very illuminating. The one word Will almost understood was "Crucifixus", but the movement's slow pulsing, its e-minor darkness, and repeated descending lines, is a very formula for putting the sleepy to sleep. And almost, almost asleep he was, into that timeless G-major space Bach had deposited him in to at the end. Peaceful, the movement's weight — even if unidentified as such — lifted off his shoulders and his soul, em-balmed him, as it were, in the balm of its tonal transformations.

A conductor has two choices here, the first being to allow that moment, though temporal, to extend out into eternity, as a bell continues to silently vibrate, or pond ripples continue to diminish and propagate. The other would be to take only the few seconds indicated by rests in the score, and then to bash the somnolent eardrum with the trumpets and voices announcing the resurrection. Et ressurexit! In other words, scare the bejeezus out of the audience, as an actual resurrection would surely do. But worst (best?) of all is to combine both — to allow the caressing silence to continue as if humanity's eternal goal had indeed, miraculously, been reached — and *then* to smash it hard as one can.

The Dutch conductor, perhaps in reflection on, or retaliation to, the recent war, took the third route, as if his very own family were involved in the torture, and then the liberation from the camps. "What did I do? I didn't do anything!" was Will's reaction. But a life-long sense of impotence and helplessness was the gift of this moment, "Gift", in German, meaning "poison". " ET RESURREXIT" was the flag he would ever try to fly.

William James wrote that "the baby, assailed by eyes, ears, nose, skin, and entrails all at once, feels it all as one great blooming, buzzing confusion."

It is clear that William James was never a baby. At least not a baby named Will, with a Superman/Schopenhauer S on his saque, an S embroidered (embroidered!) on his every diaper, an S drawn in waterproof ink on each of his rubber pants, printed on the chest of his onesies, crocheted into his every baby blanket, and appliqued onto his heirloom baby quilts.

As a baby and toddler, Will didn't feel confused at all. For instance, he heard voices while peeing. I'm not talking about hearing voices à la Joan of Arc. Just simple voices, saying simple, adult-like things about this and that. At three, he was tall enough to put his potty pot down on the floor, to stand over it like some Gulliver, posturing, fly-unzipped, in Lilliput, and to listen carefully to what it was telling him.

To demonstrate what he heard as he stood over his potty chair, you might imagine something like this:

c know the half of it how much ʋ
.t would be great if you could help. I ʋ
ʋ what it has to do with anything but I'll
hem about it. She said they couldn't come
er early. They're very nice people. yes, I'll
ve another, wake me a not you I can tell him
mething anything stay later if you can don't I
tranger that's enough for me thank you. Wh
ut him? I don't really care see you on Frida
t will you be having dinner? Who is the
est person there the dogs were
ful, that was fabulous. Really fabi
ay anything I'm in the midd
ive you any good -

This print version is much clearer than what Will actually experienced. For one thing, he heard only one word or fragment at a time, before it was replaced by the next. He couldn't go back to look at an earlier line for context, or take a moment to consider what was being said. He had to grab and remember, grab and remember, which, if you think about it, is the only way we hear music as such, and not as a simple succession of sounds. It was from peeing that Will became such a good musician. It also shows you what a great invention writing is.

BEDTIME STORIES AND SONGS

Mother Gwen, having grown up poor to non-

reading parents, had had mostly story-less bedtimes:
the occasional, self-selected, standards from the
library — Little House on the Prairie, Wee Gillis,
Doctor Doolittle. Her parents' performances were
less than perfect, and because they felt embarrassed
with themselves, bedtime stories petered out to
nothing. Until Gwen had learned to read, she had
to subsist on hand-holding, sitting with, or simple
"Good night, don't let the bedbugs bite," which she
didn't quite understand, since her parents had made
absolutely sure there were no bedbugs. She told
stories to herself.

Charles, on the other hand, had had a nanny
specifically hired for her reading and writing skills.
The Vanderbilts had recruited her not from a nanny
agency, but via their friend, the publisher Henry
Holt, who had read some of her work, and had
interviewed Lydia Barrymore, a less-famous member
of that prominent acting family, equipped, however,
with a similar set of genes.

I spoke earlier about four songs and concerts that had musically maneuvered his life. The first of those songs was comparatively small, a little ditty he'd heard on one of the radios at home, called "My heart cries for you." He already knew about crying. It was the following internal rhymes that planted a seed. "…cries for you, sighs for you, dies for you…" He really wasn't sure what sighing was, but when he asked, his mother demonstrated. Something like expelling air? No, it was more like being sorry about something, or giving up into resigned acceptance. Neither of which made things clear to a three-year old. But, ok, he could breath out as a thing, although just how a heart could do that, he'd let pass. But the sequence of crying, sighing and dying could not be ignored. What, exactly, was dying? Dying, his mother tried, was how you got dead. And what is dead? When you just lie there and can't move. Why can't you move? Because there's no "you" there. The "you" has gone away. Where does it go?

At or around this point, most secular parents will resort to the "You'll understand when you're older" gambit — which leaves most children distrusting adults until they become one, and even after. And with this distrust comes a deeply embedded sense of the upcoming agenda: cry, sigh, die. Malevolent rhyming. Talk about dangerous toys!

Bad Song Two arrived a mere two years later, when, in kindergarten, the beautiful Edith Brownwell, object of Will's affection, refused to return it. One afternoon after school, Father Charles found him lying on the parlor couch in tears over Edith's latest cruel slight. What can a child know? Rather, what can grown-ups know of these traumas, always slightly comical to them?

Charles stroked Will's hair, and brushed away the tear gliding sideways down his cheek. Inappropriate, as he often was, he froze, announced "I've got an idea", and ran to the music room, to thumb through a box of old 78s he had gathered to show those snobs at Eton just how great America was. All his father's unexpected energy caught Will up short. Charles returned with an old RCA single, Homer and Jethro's great hillbilly number, "I've got tears in my ears from lying on my back, cryin' in my pillow over you." Father and son cracked up together. At the line, "If I should get water on my brain, You will know you're the one whose to blame," Charles was able to elicit the woeful tale of Will and Edith Brownwell, or Will and not Edith Brownwell, and he recalled and shared his own story of thirty or so years earlier of his own first love, Laura something, he didn't remember her last name. Will got up, considerably drier.

But again, at what cost? For one thing, an inkling that his father was not all-powerful, all-knowing, able to protect him, when he couldn't even protect himself from a little pipsqueak Laura somebody. For another, he did have water in his left ear which he couldn't get out, and which held before him, the possibility of deafness and decay. And thirdly — his father, even as a child, in love with somebody other than his mother? All sorts of cracking in Will's porcelain stupidity. He would understand when he got older.

His third poisonous song came in junior high

school. The tax-rich Mt. Kisco public schools could afford to search for, and pay more for, better than average teachers, and one such was a Mr. Leigh Minster, the kind of wag Charles had known at Eton, here, uniquely displaced into suburban New England. It was he who introduced young Will to the word "macaronic", which strangely had little to do with actual macaroni. The poem went like this:

Amo, Amas, I love a lass
As a cedar tall and slender;
Sweet cowslip's grace is her nominative case,
And she's of the feminine gender.

Chorus:
Rorum, Corum, sunt divorum,
Harum, Scarum divo;
Tag-rag, merry-derry, periwig and hat-band
Hic hoc horum genitivo.

Can I decline a Nymph divine?
Her voice as a flute is dulcis.

Her oculus bright, her manus white,
And soft, when I tacto, her pulse is.
(Chorus)

Oh, how bella my puella,
I'll kiss secula seculorum.
If I've luck, sir, she's my uxor,
O dies benedictorum.
(Chorus)

Never mind the particular Latin words learned
(with the possible exception of "genitivo", or the
unwonted sensuality for a junior high school
mixed class. The seventeenth century poet and
playwright, John O'Keeffe, (as noted by William
Hazlett (all this in Mr. Minster's spoutings) as the
"English Molière", who "in light, careless laughter
and pleasant exaggeration of the humorous had
no equal"), remaining unknown to contemporary
Americans, gave Will his first inkling of possessing
special, secret knowledge, different from that of
others, and certainly from that of his contemporaries,

even that of the smart, rich kid friends he had
inherited. Thrilling in a way, the toxicity of unshared
knowledge is what drives spies to suicide, and
poisons friendships.

And especially when, once again, he did love a
lass as a cedar tall and slender, a love which could
not speak its name, since "loving" someone in junior
high school, was as tease-worthy as it was universal.
This lass was the unspeakably beautiful Elizabeth
Schrank, her last name, alas, descriptive of her
reaction to being pursued. And pursued she was by
any male in school who thought he might have a
chance against the pride of other young lions from
the seventh grade on. And by who knows how many
females who might desire her as display friend or
even lover.

Will's wooing was one of impassioned shyness.
He was proud of having the courage to even speak
at all — which he didn't, except to nod hello in
the halls and stairways, and once, when sharing
a short elevator trip from the school lobby to its
second floor, to actually say out loud, "Which floor?"

concerning which there was only one choice, and then to re-press the button he had already pressed for himself. To which Elizabeth Schrank said, "Thank you," in a voice and a moment he would ever treasure and dwell upon.

MONEY

And speaking of treasure, long before Liz Schrank, there was the famous piggy bank issue.

"That doesn't look like a pig! I saw a pig once," Will groused, tossing the clay beastie to the ground, and smashing it in pieces.

"It's not supposed to be realistic," his father said. "It's supposed to be cute."

"We don't like cute," Will said. He had recently taken to referring to himself in the first person plural, though Charles and Gwen weren't sure if it were just four-year old linguistic stupidity, or an actual employment of the royal we, and in any case, they thought it (his saying "we") cute.

But they had been intent on teaching him about

money, the value of money, how hard it is to get and keep it if you lived in the real world, as they hoped he would, a discussion of that particular distinction being reserved for the first grade, at least.

Had one reassembled the pieces and shards scattered poolside, one would have discovered a quite charming clay piggy bank of Mexican origin, orange in color, shaded in brown, with a strangely green nose, two small diamond eyes (likely glass), with a pink, yellow and green flower painted on each side, a large slit on its back, and, strangely, no stoppered hole in its belly for eventual withdrawal of funds. A kamikaze Mexican pig from FAO Schwartz, destined to be smashed to bits for its contents — some paradigm there for both piggy and smasher.

But piggy was no more, and Will proposed an alternative which seemed reasonable to two philosophy major parents, who had both met Wittgenstein.

"We want a real pig, not a piggy, so our bank can hold lots of money. Not an actual real pig, of course, but one that looks like a genuine, real pig without flowers on it. And we want to feed it money in its mouth, not through a slot in its back. That would kill it if it cut into its spine, and it probably couldn't walk, either."

Where he had picked up his neuro-anatomy, his parents didn't know, but there were lots of things they didn't know, and their unintended-as-such epistemological machine kept spitting out results to be enjoyed and analyzed, as the ghosts of Turing and Wittgenstein hovered, and the first Sputnik beeped overhead.

Even the piggy bank, before being smashed, did not realize that it's real name was not piggy at all but only a mis-heard, mis-spoken, or perhaps creative pun. I'm sure the reader will enjoy knowing that "pygg" is an orange-colored clay, and that money jars in Merrie Olde Engel-land were called pygg-pots. From there, the etymological track is clear. The replacement pig-sculpture bank, mouth-fed, came at high cost from a sculptor in Vermont, but with a corked hole in the belly for withdrawals, which Will pretended was its penis.

A latter part of his Economics 0.1 lessons involved discussing whether to put money into Big Swine, or to deposit it in a real bank, say, Mt. Kisco Chase Bank, whose founder, Salmon P. Chase, had been a frenemy of Charles's family, and who had been nominated to the Supreme Court by Abraham Lincoln. Lincoln was the person on Will's pennies. The problem, in brief, was that money in Big Swine just sat there, while money in a bank bank "grew". No, it didn't get bigger, there just became more of it. "How?" It made "interest". "What's interest?"

The water was thickening into mud, and the discussion grew into an argument which had components of religious war, potentially antisemitic.

In the Hebrew Bible, Ezekiel condemned growing money via "interest" — which was seen as usury, an "abominable" sin, one of the worst. Only God could create living, increasing, being. Thus the Jesus the Jew kicked money "changers" out of the temple. Thus believèd Gwen. The family delicatessen had been funded and grown through many small contributions, some eventually returned to relatives and friends.

For the Vanderbilts, the existence of interest was never an issue, only the rate of interest allowable by a like-minded government. State laws distinguish the usurious from the not, calls interest over a certain level "loan-sharking", and punishes it accordingly. The Vanderbilts played by state rule, and were often influential in making them. The federal government had never attempted to regular interstate interest rates on private business loans. The Vanderbilts, like the feds, saw nothing essentially wrong with "interest".

Even two philosophy majors, one Jewish, ex-poor, one Catholic, ever-rich, did not see the need to straighten all this out in the court of a four-year old. Still, the pillow talk that night was complex and less-than-friendly, and man and wife slept back to back, each on their own side of the king-size Louis Quinze four-poster bed.

Putting Childish Things Aside

Two years passed, during which Will, with an ever-growing understanding of society and its workings, decided to become an emancipated child, apply for welfare, to be an adult for legal purposes, and to marry or form a corporate partnership with Naomi, a girl in his 1st grade class. It was time to put aside childish things.

Actually, the Naomi affair was quite complex, beginning with Will's attempt to secretly poison a bunny with fish flakes stolen from his kitchen cabinet, his investigation spoiled in advance by his mis-translation of *poisson*. Naomi, his once-co-conspirator, had decided to spill the beans to Miss Mellert, his first grade teacher, the owner, or possibly short-term borrower of said bunny for pedagogical purposes. I wouldn't like to have been a bunny selected to help the children "learn to care responsibly for living things".

Will's experiment in bunnycide stemmed from a recent visit, in the company of his parents, to the Metropolitan Opera, Will's second encounter with his old friend from *Firebird*, the demon, Kashchey the Deathless, this time starring in his own opera, Rimsky-Korsakoff's *Kashshey the Deathless*. In Will's

mind it was pretty garbled stuff — that opera —
but it did require and provoke some real-world
exploration. What did it take to poison someone to
death and release love from the loveless daughter of
Kaschey, Kascheyevna?

The someone was easy: he could kill the bunny,
and in terms of getting in trouble, who would know,
except him? It could have been any of the other
twelve kids in his class. Or natural bunny causes.
Miss Mellert would never know for sure. It was a
setup for the perfect crime.

Releasing love from the loveless? That was more
difficult. But perhaps his experiment was here, too,
at hand. For who, in fact, seemed more loveless than
Naomi Billington, the girl he wanted to marry?

Any first year psychiatry student, not to mention
any Chinese doctor adept at visual diagnosis,
would have immediately recognized an anhedonic,
dysphoric, dyspeptic young girl, headed straight
for an unhappy adolescence, and possibly hospital
or prison thereafter. That is, if they didn't take
into account that her father was president of Mt.

Kisco Federal Savings, and her family descended from John and Eleanor Billington, who, with their two sons, John and Francis, made up four of the 102 passengers on the Mayflower. (This was not just rumor. The Billingtons had the documents to prove it. If Naomi were to be firmly diagnosed as anhedonic, dysphoric, and dyspeptic, what would that say about America and its genes?)

Will, like anyone within six feet of Naomi, was aware of this diagnosis in his own terms: ("She never laughs or even smiles, and during recess, never plays"), but Will, unlike anyone else in his class, had seen both the beginning of *Kashchey the Deathless*, and also the end, the liberation and transformation of the once anhedonic, dysphoric, etc. Kashchey's daughter, Kascheyevna, as only the Metropolitan Opera could present it, and from up close in the family box, using his own opera glasses, which he called binoculars. If Kashchey's daughter could open up and laugh and cry, so could Mr. and Mrs. Billington's daughter, no? Or at least go along with this experiment?

Naomi did, and with her special version of glee. While Will brought the *poisson* flakes from home, it was she that sprinkled them liberally into the bunny cage. Because Naomi was a "special" student, tentatively mainstreamed into a "normal" class, Miss Mellert kept her wanderings under close watch, and called a halt to the goings-on, whatever they were.

Naomi had been caught red-handed, but where did she get the fish-smelling bunny food? "Someone gave it to me," was all she'd give up, the dear. But as a result of expert grilling and the pseudo-science of elimination, it was Will that was finally focused on, and Will who finally confessed to his researches — in terms no first-grade teacher could possibly understand. Something about love and compassion and someone turning into a willow tree.

Miss Mellert came down hard (for Miss Mellert) on the would-be killer: she called Will's parents in for a visit, a rare event at Mt. Kisco Elementary, where class issues were generally pursued downward, and mere teachers, most often female, did their best to stroke, and not annoy, the haute-bourgeoisie and above.

Was there any harm done to the bunny? Mr. and Mrs. Vanderbilt wanted to know. No. Could there have been any harm done to the bunny by what Will and Naomi had done? No. What, then, is the issue? Intention. What were Will and Naomi's intentions? That was what Miss Mellert was curious about. Mr. and Mrs. Vanderbilt listened to Miss Mellert's garbling of Will's garbled exposition, and while they recognized the phrase Somebody the Deathless, they could only throw up their hands along with those of Miss Mellert. That made six hands.

It turns out that bunnies — at least this one — loved fish flakes, and that discovery henceforth lightened Miss Mellert's burden in keeping various bunnies happy, semester after semester. So the result of the whole affair was labeled positive, and Will was commended for his animal husbandry, and publicly honored at a weekly school assembly. Resurrexit. I don't mean to be ironic. The fact is that he had imbibed, called forth, and executed information from deep in folkloric pre-history. How many first-graders could have done that?

Will decided to break up with Naomi, since she had gotten him in trouble by not being subtle enough in her sprinkling, and because she was too dour. Conveniently, Naomi decided to break up with Will, since they were never together in the first place, and since he was an asshole, getting her to do his dirty work for him. Boys. They were like that. She must have been really angry, since Will was the last boy she was ever with — even though she wasn't. Her future novel, *The Peninsula of Lesbos* (Harper Rowe, 1986), was praised by Susan Sontag, in the *New York Review of Books*, as "entirely original, a breakthrough work of enormous discernment." You never know.

As part of putting childish things aside, and to mark his graduation from Fieldstone Lower to Fieldston Middle division, Will asked that he become financially semi-independent, and instead of living off his family's immense fortune, that he receive an allowance, and be forced to acknowledge and live within its limitations.

Love and Death, though, were hardly off the agenda, and were only waiting in the wings for their re-entrance during the next Vanderbilt-Davidoff family heritage tour: Mama's family had coursed through Austria, Bohemia, and later, Germany.

In November of 1961, [Will, age 12] the Vanderbilt's heritage tour had taken them to Munich, where they were pleased to discover (the effect on Will as yet unsuspected) that the famous Tonhalle would be celebrating the fiftieth anniversary of its premier of Mahler's *das Lied von der Erde*, the composer's unsuccessful attempt to evade the death that seems to accompany all great symphonists upon completion of their Ninth Symphony. "I've done my Eighth. I have a serious heart condition. If I write a Ninth, I'll surely die. So I won't write a Ninth. I'll write a set of orchestral songs instead." His reasoning and reference frame was no doubt more complex, but this was the gist of it. After writing *das Lied*, he would write his next symphony — what the world now calls his Ninth. Death was not so stupid as to be fooled. Mahler died shortly afterward. He never got to hear the songs or the Ninth be performed.

Given the circumstances, and whatever Mahler's intentions, *das Lied von der Erde* was bound to give off a deathy fragrance. Its final song, longer than the earlier five movements combined, was titled *der Abschied*, the leave-taking, the farewell. Again, not music for most impressionable, lanky, dark-haired, large-eyed, twelve-year olds.

The first of the six songs is called *Das Trinklied vom Jammer der Erde*, the *Drinking Song of the Sorrow of the Earth*. The first oddity is why the Sorrow of the Earth would be written as a drinking song at all, and not a song of mourning or lamentation. But the 10th century Chinese poet lived in a world different from ours. The second strangeness is the song's ferocity, when what it finally comes down to is "*Dunkel ist das Leben, ist der Tod* — dark is life, is death. But the most curious thing of all is its penultimate image:

Seht dort hinab! Im Mondschein auf den Gräben
Hockt eine wild-gespenstische Gestalt —

Ein Aff' ist's! Hort ihr, wie sein Heulen
Hinausgellt in den süssen Duft des Lebens!

Look down there! In the moonlight on the graves
a wild-ghostly shape is crouching —
It's an ape! Listen to how its howling
rings out into the sweet fragrance of life!

So have some wine! It's time, friends.
Drain your cup to the dregs!
Dunkel ist das Leben...

Now if that isn't strange, I don't know what is. Darwin
wouldn't be born for a thousand years. But Will, who
didn't drink, didn't smoke, didn't do drugs, took it as
only natural.

As he did John Kennedy's assassination, two years
after the family's Munich trip. He knew the official
story was ridiculous. No bullet from the rear could
have blown the president's occiput back out of his
head toward the shooting rifle. That, and a hundred

other impossible details were obvious to fourteen-year old. But he attended a progressive school in a progressive town. He read the NY Times, but he also read Upton Sinclair, and Sinclair Lewis, and Steinbeck, and *Ramparts* and Izzy Stone, while the *Weekly* was still publishing.

He knew about the CIA, and Hoover's FBI, and the Cuban missile crisis, the domino theory, and Kennedy's anti-communism in Vietnam. Dunkel ist das Leben ist der Tod.

The Evolution of S

He knew about all this because he was a sophisticated kid, early branded by the Superman S on his onesie. But he never left the S behind. You may be surprised, but Joe Schuster's 1938 red S tapering toward the point of an inverted, red-bordered yellow triangle had since become one of the most recognized logos in the world, and has been used, licensed or stolen, on almost every imaginable class of product, from stationary and

business cards to pocket knives, medicine balls,
and auto-body wraps. Having begun the S gag, his
parents continued to perpetrate it throughout his
toddler and child years, and their S-identified son
continued it on his own, with some combination
of ironic self-deprecation, and pompous arrogance.
As Swami Vivekananda said: "The greatest sin is to
think yourself weak."

In Will's iconology, the "S"s he often wore,
referred now and then to Stravinsky, Schoenberg,
Schubert, Schumann, Scarlatti, Schütz, Satie,
Stockhausen, Strauss (R.), Shostakovich, Sibelius,
and even some minor-league players such as Johann
Schein and Samuel Scheidt.

You may notice that all of the above are
composers. So what happened to the Three B's
— four, perhaps five, if you count Bela Bartok?
Although acknowledged, they were simply
eliminated by virtue of their last initials. An
admittedly strange way to pick a path through
the forest of western music, but Will had to use
some principle to guide his music history lessons

at Fieldston Upper, his weekend afternoons in the listening booths at Sam Goody's.

Why composers? Did Will even sing or play an instrument? Lest we lose track of the plot here, Will, child of two philosophes, student at a "gifted" school, from a pre-precocious age was aware of Schopenhauer's understanding of music as standing quite apart from all the other arts.

In it we do not recognize the copy, the repetition, of any Idea of the inner nature of the world. Yet it is such a great and exceedingly fine art, its effect on man's innermost nature is so powerful, and it is so completely and profoundly understood by him in his innermost being as an entirely universal language, whose distinctness surpasses even that of the world of perception itself...

Why had he not taken music lessons, though his parents could certainly afford them? Because he thought any particular instrument, even the piano (a percussion instrument!) too limiting, too devouring of the whole in its particularities, in effect, too destructive of the music it produced (we're dealing with some strange, Willish intertangulations here).

Why had he not taken up composition or conducting? Because what chutzpah it would be to compete with the GREATS (that's all capital letters), or to force his necessarily trivial interpretations on other musicians!

Though one might suspect some rationalization here, cloaking a fear of inadequacy or failure, the fact was that Will really meant all this: his humility was on a par with his arrogance, both deeply sincere. And music, above all, was their field of play.

By the way, Stravinsky or Schoenberg notwithstanding, Superman's S, is a registered trademark, ®. Privately, mentally, you may assign any meaning to it you like, but put it on an object for public consumption — well, even Superman has lawyers.

It was at an Easter party at the Vanderbilt house, some time in the late fifties, one heavily populated by lawyers, that Will first heard the good news about Jesus rising from the dead. Or was it good news? That remained to be seen. Of course it was mentioned only in jest, something about "but if he comes out in 3 days and sees his shadow there's going to be six more weeks of winter."

This story can raise many questions in a curious, eavesdropping mind. I need not list them. But chief among them is whether someone can actually be dead, and then alive again, strong enough to push a boulder out from the mouth of a cave. Young Will remembered the howling ape sitting on a tombstone, except this time the ape was Jesus, sitting on the boulder he had just moved, beating his chest like the ape in the movie his parents had mistakenly taken him to and regretted, and half-singing-half-howling about resurrection. What *was* resurrection? Did it have anything to do with erections, a subject of recent and intense interest?

And then there was that Christmas party for which Charles had hired Julian Bream, a famous lutenist he had met in England during their student days. Mr.

Bream had sung and played a very curious song about a "virgin unspotted". Will thought he knew what a virgin was, or at least he had heard of a virgin named Mary, but were there two types of virgins, some with spots and some without? The other part of the song he remembered even more clearly — that is, he didn't remember *it*, exactly, but rather the audience joining joyously, ferociously, in on four words,

> *to be our redeemer from*
> *DEATH, HELL, AND SIN*
> *which our transgressions*
> *involv-ed us in.*

And what about "transgressions"? They seemed perhaps more problematic than those erections on Easter. Still, there was a happy ending:

> *Then let us be merry,*
> *put sorrow away,*
> *Our savior, Christ Jesus,*
> *was born on this day.*

Happy, at least, as long as you didn't worry too much about "savior". At which, for some strange reason, his mother began to cry, and quickly left the living room to hide her tears, Will following behind her. "What's the matter, Mom?" Crying and laughing at the same time, she confided, "I really want a knish." True story.

Will should probably not attend his parents' parties, at least after they got going.

But

My Heart Cries For You, I've Got Tears In My Ears, even *Amo, Amas I Love a Lass* — these were all kid stuff. The fourth song to assault poor Will introduced a whole new dimension. His first high school musical was the perpetrator. *South Pacific.* This race-haunted, but relatively death-free, portrayal of World War II. Who would have thunk it?

Enter a girl dainty as a sparrow, and where narrow, as narrow as an arrow — and then the kicker: "and she's broad where a broad should be braw-awaw-aw-aw-awed". Several confusing things about this. One: what really is a broad? The word had never been used in the Vanderbilt house, nor likely in all Mt. Kisco, nor at Fieldston Middle before this. Something to do with a girl, but what exactly? But worst of all, why is she talking — even singing — in public about something Will had been thinking, but keeping his cards ever so close to his chest? It was as if he were being exposed as the sex-hungry fiend he was, outed, as we might say today. Just thinking about that combination of narrowness and broadness made him blush.

The carrier of these dimensions was his classmate ("mate"!) one Lucy Griffin, the daughter of some left-wing City College Professor who 15-year old Will had actually heard of, and was already scared of meeting. The *South Pacific* song eerily described her: waist and hips, check. She was definitely petite — a hundred and one pounds of fun, plus or minus a pound or two. She was sixty inches high, right up to Will's shoulder, with curly blond hair, and something

— two things — the song had not mentioned, projecting from her chest.

Will knew that she knew that he knew. But so what? She had been a woman for far longer than he had been a man. And what does a woman have to do with a boy, especially one with a Superman logo on his backpack? While not actually needing to pick up a girl in his own class, he felt he needed some kind of pickup line to get their relationship rolling at a different clip. His "When I was ten, I had a philosophical breakthrough" did not prompt a "What?" Nor did his critique of the unintelligent design of male-female relations elicit an interested response. His "Most people around here despise me" did call forth a head nod. But his invitation to join a Death Book Club, and his signup sheet for a to-be-organized École Normale Inférieure, or a New York Society for the Suppression of Death remained empty not only of her signature, but of any other student's at Fieldston Middle. Apparently, at 15, most students from rich, progressive families are into death.

What did get her was a free ticket to the Amato Opera's Tristan. Free. She did not know that all performances were free, because Actor's Equity and American Federation of Musicians rules prohibited charging money when using an unpaid cast. What she also didn't know was that the Amato Opera was not the Met, but rather a tiny East Village company shoehorned into a 300 seat theater (the Met holds 4000) , itself shoehorned into the 100s block of Bleeker Street. Nevertheless, the Amato was no shabby little operation, but a renowned testing ground and development space for young singers, many of whom went on to major careers in opera companies around the world. The seating capacity was small, but the experience of grand opera in an intimate space was remarkable, even for seasoned Met subscribers, with whom the audience was often filled. The young singers looked good: no love duets between fatsos with triple chins and thick waists.

First performed in 1865, it is hard to match up the thirteenth century world of *Tristan* with Abraham Lincoln, the Civil War, and the abolition of slavery. Yet they share many of the basic themes as always emerge in standout moments: life and death, love and betrayal, landscapes of darkness and landscapes of light.

Culturally sophisticated as she was, Lucy Griffin's first reaction to the daylight scene on ship was to love being able to look up the singers' nostrils, where hairs waved back and forth like sea grass on the beaches of Cornwall. An imaginative focus. Will was amazed at her interest and perspicacity. But in the night-drenched second act, one could barely see the actors, much less their nostril hairs. You certainly knew they were there, for they were belting it out louder and more weirdly than ever.

When I say weirdly, I mean weirdly. The score to the love duet in the second act might be a tracking of worms and amoebas slithering over one another in the darkness of mud. The direction seemed mostly downwards. But there is only so far you can go downwards, before downwards becomes upwards — especially given two aspiring young opera singers slash death-drunk lovers, being goosed continually by Richard Wagner, and unleashed in darkness. There were no melodies, no sequences evolved predictably, no note ever landed where one expected it might. Any ear raised on and used to the implications of centuries of Western harmony was wrestled to the mat, further battered, and squooshed into the ground. Once in, you couldn't get out, and the kneading and twisting of the dough-mass-that-was-you seemed as if it would never stop. Resistance was futile, escape impossible. What fiendish mind had devised such harrowing torture? Reinhard Heydrich? No wonder Hitler loved Wagner. If such is love, let us be loveless! Let us rather embrace the nostril hairs.

Will loved Lucy Griffin all the more for her reaction. It was not something he could tell her. They got through all four hours of it, four and a half, counting intermissions. She would never speak to him afterwards.

Perhaps to demonically protect himself, he bought a white sweatshirt and in place of his normal Superman S, he carefully inscribed with fabric crayon the famous "Tristan Chord" upon it. He found it on the cover notes to the Furtwängler recording. His classmates were shocked. This was a new Will. If he was calling down new superpowers, no one knew what they were. And he wasn't telling, since he didn't know himself, and couldn't have.

A word about that strange, most goyish tetragrammaton,

YHVH no more, but now FBD#G#, the very sharpness of those sharps imaging the thorns on Christ's crown. It does make a good, non-conversation-starting sweatshirt logo.

Unlike most leading chords in Western harmony, those that cue the Western ear correctly, the Tristan Chord leads *somewhere*, but does not seek resolution. It just stands there unresolved, sufficient unto itself without being final.

The blasé music professor might say, "Oh, that's

just an augmented fourth, augmented sixth, and augmented ninth above an F, or above any bass note." But there's no music professor or musician that would not recognize it as "the Tristan Chord", as any artist would recognize the Mona Lisa, or any architect, the Parthenon. It may have occurred earlier, somewhere, in passing, but never before as a standing object of contemplation. After its measure 2 appearance, it poses again, in different pitches, four more times, like a bird flying up from branch to branch, or perhaps the first of Hitchcock's birds settling itself upon a tree.

Will's putting childish things aside by living within an allowance was more difficult than he had imagined. Although the allowance was generous, his spending habits were even more so. For example, after the annual tire repair lesson, using his birthday take, he would indulge in a tool-buying spree at Mt. Kisco Truck and Auto Parts, "Good guys helping people get stuff done", which, in spite of its deplorable rhythm as a slogan, was quite true, as its customer comments have shown for half a century. While fulfilling its titular function, its general hardware section was likely the best in Westchester, and by the time Will graduated to Fieldstone Upper, the red, rolling tool cabinet in his parents' garage was stocked with more tools than that of most professional, full-time mechanics, certainly more than he would ever use. He liked tools. He liked their looks, he liked their solidity, even if he didn't know what they did, or what they were for. As I say, his spending habits were generous. And you will notice that this rich store of implements, will implement almost nothing.

But this footnotes only the spending-side of Will's striving and spending. He was, if nothing else, a striver, needed money for his tools, and lately his classical record collection, and was a perfect Thomas Edison of inventive entrepreneurial thought.

The history of the Wisdom Bagel™, short-lived though it may have been, had a complex history chez Vanderbilt. It begins with Will pushing his first no-training-wheels "two-wheeler", a top of the line Schwinn 24" beauty, with white-wheel tires, a headlight on its front fender, and a tank with a button for its built-in horn. Up the steps and onto the Persian rug where he dumped it in front of his father. "It's broken!" he lamented. "It's not broken," Charles said. "It looks like it just has a flat tire." "Well, how am I supposed to ride it?" Will angrily demanded.

There followed a perfectly lovely, perfectly horrible father-son half hour which involved fetching the tool box, removing the front wheel with the right size wrench, levering the tire off its rim with a screwdriver, removing the nail with a pliers, finding the hole in the inner tube by pumping it up in the bathtub, drying the tub, peeling and gluing on a tire patch, and applying a band-aid to a cut, washed, and mercurochromed five-year-old knuckle. A very high-density learning experience on both sides. It was the pumped-up tube, blowing its slight stream of bubbles in the bath tub, that started the whole thing: Will had been introduced to the torus.

A mathematical torus is a shape generated by rotating a circular surface head-on, 360 around a central pivot. Hold a quarter around its rim, arm straight out, and turn once around. That quarter will have carved a torus out of space. Toroids hold much interest for solid geometrists. And even for Will, entirely innocent of Euclid or Descartes.

That evening, Will went to his mother, who no longer cooked but owned a library of illustrated cook books, and asked her if she could make an edible torus. Plowing through the "You, know it's like when you…" attempt at description, she immediately grasped what he was getting at. Her inner daughter of the Lower East Side immediately summoned up a bagel. "What's a bagel?" Their physical descriptions coincided. Tomorrow, she and he would play in the kitchen, and try to create a few. Father and son, now mother and son. All that was lacking was Norman Rockwell, and, had they thought of it, they could have commissioned him for some not insignificant fee.

Will got into making bagels for a while, but since they involved mixing and kneading and boiling and baking, bagel-making was quickly too much for the household help to put up with, and bagel production soon stopped. Or rather, it went into a long hibernation through elementary and middle-school,

only to be resurrected, fully toothed and haired, as
the famous, if again short-lived, Wisdom Bagels™,
of Fieldstone Upper. The "TM" did not represent
any legal work or protection, but only a kind of sweet
dedication to his mom, for showing him how.

It was clearly an idea whose time had long come.
Lao Tsu might have opened a Wisdom Bagel business
back in 556 BC, when he was Will's age. But with
the atom bomb almost twenty years old now, the
twentieth century had to somewhat make up for such
brainy brainlessness, hence Wisdom Bagels™.

Here's how Will did it: the Stage II bagels
were removed from the boiling water after having
expanded, and the Wisdoms were inserted by folding
the Wisdom slips in quarters, then using a butter
knife to push the folded message into the dough. The
wound was then pinched together, brushed lightly
with egg wash, and the enriched bagel went into the
oven for Stage III.

That was the obvious part. What wasn't so easy
was coming up with Wisdoms. To make things less
eclectic and more forceful, Will decided to proceed

one Wisdomthinker at a time, beginning with his
semi-namesake, Schopenhauer. But the very first
slip, inserted in a special bagel he himself kept, the
Prelude Bagel, contained this:

— the famous prelude to Tristan, the bearer of
the Tristan Chord.

The richness of this object will outlast this
telling (as bagels, almost indestructible, will outlast
their bakers): the mix of pagan, Christian and
Jew, the love of Tristan and Isolde, along with the
antisemitism of Wagner, the simultaneous chewiness
and ineffability, the torus, and its mathematical
distortion during its manufacture, the daylight of
common bagel consumption, and the dark night in
which the Wisdom slips had slept.

As for the following Schopenhauerian set of wisdoms, the problem was one of surfeit, and of finding stand-alone Wisdoms to fit in short, rectangular shapes, not Schopenhauer's favorite format.

Will's first ten grabs were as follows:

— When modesty was made a virtue, it was a very advantageous thing for fools, for everyone is expected to speak of himself as if he were one.

— *Fame is something which must be won; honor only something which must not be lost.*

— *The chief sign that a man has any nobility in his character is the little pleasure he takes in others' company.*

— *A reproach can only hurt if it hits the mark.*

— *National character is only another name the littleness, perversity, and baseness of mankind takes in every country.*

— *For our improvement, we need a mirror.*

— *Mostly it is loss which teaches us about the worth of things.*

— *Philosophy of religion really amounts to philosophizing on assumptions that are not confirmed at all."*

—The fundament upon which all our knowledge and learning rests is the inexplicable.

— Suicide may also be regarded as an experiment — a question which man puts to Nature, trying to force her to answer.

(...none of them very pleasant. Why did they name Will after his book?)

The next problem was one of materials: what things could be put in food whose seepings would not make it inedible. Will was not concerned with FDA standards, but with making bagels that would have customers coming back for more.

First, the substrate. Paper, parchment, dried chicken skin? While the latter is edible, it is messy to trim, and might not easily take ink. How edible is paper? Not so much the paper itself, which would be looked at, digested only mentally, then discarded. But what might be seeping out of the paper? And what kind of paper? Plain, unlined, notebook paper? Letter paper? Wrapping paper, butcher paper? What *was* butcher paper? How did it keep the blood in? And how did wrapping paper keep the rain out? Since it was traditionally used in contact with food, Will thought butcher paper the best bet. But all the meat he had ever seen in stores was bedded in styrofoam and wrapped in plastic. Did butcher paper still exist? Where were there butcher stores in Mt. Kisco? On his European heritage tours he had seen papeteries. But in Mt. Kisco? The butcher in the Mt. Kisco A&P gave him a large tear-off of butcher paper for his experiments, enough a year's worth of Wisdoms. Worse come to worst, he could blame it on the butcher.

And then, the ink. Clearly one wouldn't want to gulp down a bottle of Parker Quink. But what then? Food coloring! He had heard of that, but would it be dark enough to purvey difficult Wisdoms? And what color? Red, he thought, to emphasize the importance of the thought. He could load up his father's fountain pen with red food coloring, and if there were trouble, he could blame it on McCormick red dye #2 being sold as edible.

The sad part was that though he had paper enough for hundreds of Wisdoms, as much ink as he needed, and flour and pots which could turn out an eternity of bagels, his enthusiasm waned before using up his first ten Wisdoms. It seemed no one at school really wanted to ingest Wisdom Bagels™ made by the hands of someone who habitually wore Superman clothing, and whose innovative ideas were always several steps ahead of normality. He ate half of his own first products, pinned the five Wisdoms to his bulletin board, and tossed the rest. Being only half-Jewish, he didn't actually like bagels all that much. What he did like was girls, especially girls that didn't much like him, and in this he was more tenacious.

Before there were INCELs, there were involuntary celibates. Will was one of them. He was not naive about developmental theory — all he had to do was look around. The girls at Fieldston Upper were women. They had started menstruating two or three or five years ago. What had Will begun two or three or five years ago? Sprouting a fews pubic hairs?

Big deal. His voice was still negotiating between
soprano and contralto. He might go fetching
around Middle school pupils. But they were little
girls in comparison, and going out with little girls
was old-lech reprehensible. A more satisfactory
solution might be for Fieldston to simply hold boys
back: double the sixth grade, double the seventh
and eighth, so upper level first years were similarly
developed. Fieldston believed in ethical "hands-
on learning". Well, what were first year Uppers
supposed to *ethically* put their hands on? Little hands
do not engage well with big tits, nor do big hands
adequately caress tiny peenies. Before Fieldston
could meet its students "where they were at", the
students had to be at similar developmental places
or there would be curricular chaos. First year Upper
boys two to three years older than first year Upper
girls would be the answer.

And it is not as if Fieldston boys would tread
water in their three repeating years. They could study
Plato and Aristotle in 6A, and Kant and Spinoza
in 6B. Or elementary physics in 7A, and quantum

mechanics in 7B. Et cetera. Fieldston would gather three more years of tuition from each male student. Who would complain?

Not the students, who, playing student in an educational wonderland, would be better equipped for their amorous and professional futures.

Not their parents, who could pay for it, or land a scholarship, and would be giving their precious children a pre-college education unique in all the world.

Not the school, who would be more than one hundred thousand bucks richer per, have lots of boasting rights, and continuous coverage in the education press.

Will wrote all this up in a well-argued essay (in Latin, in the style of Horace), for "Inklings", Fieldston Upper's literary magazine. But as is often the case, although no one would complain, no one would actually do anything about it, and so first-year Upper INCELS dominated the population, while earlier-developed boys made away with the cream of the crop.

So, alas, Will was Will the Incel, or at least, in
his time, Will the Weirdo, very scaredo, unpreparedo
for successful sexual conquest. Given his class
schedule, he left the campus as often as possible.
He traveled, by bus, then train to Penn Station, and
walked back up from 34th St. to 49th St., to the
small, but fabled-among-penniless-music-students
Sam Goody's, a record store that offered not only
steep discounts, but several listening rooms in which
customers were trusted to play possible purchases
without scratching or damaging them.

One of the less-heralded, but still significant,
catastrophes of modernity was the shrink-wrapping
of everything that might be shrink-wrapped, LP
records being one of them. Yes, one could still see the
beautifully designed covers, and read the small print
information on the back of the album — an activity
which educated no end of musical youth in the 50s
and early 60s. But what hexed them soon enough
was the shrink wrap which ended sampling of, or
simply freebie listening to the whole new world of
hi-fidelity music recording.

Many people recall the iconic moment in Mike Nichols' film, *The Graduate*, where its young hero is urged to seriously consider one word — plastics. "There is a great future in plastics." Yup.

It was sold to retailers as "flexible protective, transparent packaging", and it was exactly what poor music students did not need encasing the LPs they had come to count on as the music they could "sample" to their hearts' content, and learn the literature. Will's listening room adventures occurred just before — and at the beginning of shrink wrap. In one nationwide blow, an entire wing of education was shut down. There was no serious student listener — Will among them — who did not feel the slamming door.

Yes, he could have pursued almost any listening agenda in the extensive collection at Fieldston Upper, but it was Fieldston Upper, and a certain person, that he was trying to avoid. The music, once secondary to his flight, became primary to his plan for death and resurrection. And as we know, it was not anything literal, like Strauss' *Death and Transfiguration* that snagged him in, but the less-to-the-point, more implicative Tristan Chord. Therein, somehow, lay the solution to the infuriating Lucy Griffin.

Will had ever been the experimental scientist, exploring new paths as he encountered them. Back in the Kaschey the Deathless days, and intrigued with the story of cats having nine lives, he renamed Mieze, his cat, Kitty the Deathless. He gave the new identity a couple of weeks to stick, and when his parents began calling Mieze "KtD", he understood the transformation as achieved. Then he dropped her out of a third story window right onto the slate walkway around the pool. As an of unintended cherry-on-top, she bounced, staggered, and tumbled into the pool. Et resurrexit. She was rescued by the gardener, and ever afterward eyed Will with suspicion. The story does not end here…

Picking a College

…and certainly not before we vicariously attend to Will's choice of where he'd like to go to college.

Not *if* he'd like to go, but *when* he would inform his parents of his choice.

They reminded them that he would of course be welcome as a legacy student at Cornell, to guarantee which they had last year contributed a significant amount of money to endow the Davidoff Chair in Comparative Religion, mom standing in for both of them since "Vanderbilt" did not look very good — at least in the mid-sixties — on a named position. But since he was determined to avoid treading in his parents' footsteps, he turned legacy admission emphatically down.

Where then? He would let them know.

At first he'd considered Naropa, a Buddhist-inspired, but nonsectarian, school, centering around teaching and learning that integrates Eastern wisdom studies, and the arts, with traditional Western scholarship. But after careful reading of their catalogue, he decided they were frauds, and that he'd much prefer mindlessness to their slogan mindfulness. Wasn't that what Buddha counseled, getting rid of monkey mind, liberation from mind, and its endless cycle of deaths and rebirths and attaining the one, Mu, the great "without"? Wasn't that Schopenhauer's scheme, backing up against the wall to allow the Will to pass him by? No, a major in mindfulness was not for Will. He would apply to St. John's College, a small school in Annapolis, Maryland, where he might breathe the sea air while attending its famous Great Books Program, a complete overdosing of mind with minds until all arguments and distinctions were dissolved as one "great" contradicted another. He would go there so as to be completely unprepared for real life, and thus immune to its pathologies. His parents might not follow his logic here, but "Great Books Program" sounded as if it might be defended to any skeptical friends.

To celebrate his decision, he would hold a special service, at 11PM on November 1, partying in his room with other weirdos at Fieldston, to acknowledge the Day of the Dead. He was looking forward to the advertised first text of the Program: Aeschylus' *Agamemnon*, the king returning from the

Trojan war, murdered by his wife and her lover. That sounded pretty hot.

I hope the reader does not conclude from this that Will was some kind of Ted Bundy homicidal maniac. Re: dropping the cat, he, as usual, had done his homework, had read and noted many stories of cats surviving far greater falls (as did KtD). And he was especially nice to her afterward, Good kitty! But that cat experiment prefigured a more significant one, the one that led Randy, Jim, and Lamont, of Mt. Kisco's Dignity Funeral Home and Services to scurry for those bags of roadway salt to weigh down an empty coffin.

As with the Wisdom Bagels™, and confronted with the same indifference, Will soon lost interest in his Lucy Griffin project, and was ready to take on an even more complex, interracial, inter-cultural one.

To set this in context, let me remind the reader that ten years before Will's birth, and in the same year as the Paul Robeson Peekskill riot seared in Charlie

Vanderbilt's memory, the Daughters of the American Revolution had excluded Marion Anderson from singing at Constitution Hall via a "whites only" clause in its rental contract. Almost a quarter of a century later, Martin Luther King Jr. still had to give his "I have a dream" speech to 250,000 civil rights supporters calling for an end to racism in the United States. And in the following year, with the blood of Medgar Evers and JFK still drying, Lyndon Johnson would sign the Civil Rights Act of 1964, which act did not prevent the murders of the students James Chaney, Michael Schwerner, and Andrew Goodman, and the assassinations of Malcolm X, RFK and MLK himself. Will's last years at Fieldston Upper were seeped in this bloodfest.

And naturally, the Imp of the Perverse would offer up, as incoming third year Middle, a charming 14-year old Bella Hemings, (oh no!, the bella puella from the macaronic past...) for all anyone knew, but wouldn't ask, the great-great-great-great(-great?) grand daughter of Sally Hemings, the chief exemplar of Jeffersonian democracy.

Bella's father was John Hemings, captain of the *Atlantis*, the research vessel of the Woods Hole Oceanographic Institution up on the Cape, a 142-foot, steel-hulled ketch, the first American ship built specifically for research in marine biology, geology, and physical oceanography. A serious guy, authoritative, and black. Her mother was Katrine Phillips, CEO of Chez Katrine, a former golf pro, then-chair of the board of the NY Public Library, and quite pale-white.

Little Bella was thus a very light café-au-lait almost-woman, who turned out to be the fireball, unimpeachable, leader of the first student strike in Fieldston School history, Lower, Middle, or Upper.

In case you never heard of it...

The Fieldston School for Ethical Culture, was a product of the Ethical Culture movement founded back in the 1870s by Felix Adler, a not-so-happy eagle. The son of the rabbi of Temple Emanu-El, Felix's first sermon at his father's great Fifth Avenue synagogue turned out to be also his last. The wealthy congregants were not interested in his "Judaism of

the Future", or his claim that the existence of God
was unprovable, or that Judaism itself was simply
a notion of morality not particularly Jewish, but
embracing the whole world, Jewish, Christian,
Muslim, or atheist. The only faith needed, Felix
Adler claimed, was faith in humanity.

With ideas like that, his congregation thought it
might be better to terminate his ministry, and ship
him up to Ithaca and Cornell, where he became a
popular professor whose religious ideas embraced
labor struggles and power politics. When (inevitably)
fired by the university, Felix devoted himself to
birthing the Ethical Culture Society.

The Fieldston School, feather in Ethical
Culture's cap, pioneered the turn of the (20th)
century thought that all children — including
those of the poor — should have access to quality
schooling, bringing together moral, psychological,
and societal dimensions into what we understand
today as "progressive education". Just before the
depression, the school expanded from its earlier
home on Central Park West onto a wooded campus

in the upper reaches of the northwestern Bronx. Ethical learning, academic excellence, and "student-centered, discussion-based learning" offered the students "the freedom to make mistakes."

Right. The previous year, some parents of those students — a liberal, generous, generally high-achieving group — had been upset at the reported remarks of a social studies teacher concerning Israel. Some had even requested his dismissal, and dismissed he was. Ethical Culture's "deed not creed" in action. The students were all revved up, and ready to go.

And in Will's first Upper year, go they did. Putting in practice Felix Adler's "deed, not creed" approach to error, a small number (five) of the 20% of Fieldston Upper that were "non-caucasian", Bella Hemings among them, locked themselves into the administration building to protest what they claimed was a racist school culture. Any administrative or faculty denial, protestation, or argument just proved their assertions.

Parents were naturally upset. Sensing a no-win situation, the school agreed to increase minority hiring and non-white student acceptance, foregoing the standard SATs, which admittedly selected against non-caucasian and immigrant students, and give up prospective student interviews, including application fees, for those whose family incomes were less than $20,000 ($34,000 today). More progressive feathers in Fieldston's well-off, already well-feathered cap. Which brings us approximately back to the ellipsis, and the dropped and resurrected cat.

As we know, " ET RESURREXIT" was the flag Will would ever try to march beneath. That flag flew high at Fieldston Upper. But march with five students claiming racism barricaded in the administration building, demanding negotiations, Will's unknowing sweetheart among them??

The negotiations were particularly painful for Will. His secret beloved was locked in Admin. Who knew but she might be hungry, even starving, or invaded by Riverdale or State Police, manhandled, slapped around, even raped for punishment? She might regret her initial oomph, or like some Raskolnikova, become even more convinced of her superiority. She might find a new, more activist boyfriend. Where was ET RESURREXIT now? Will had to rescue her.

It was not only at home that Will collected tools. But what he had here at school were only thises and thats he used for art class, to make the tool-sculptures for which he had become famous. Yet, one artwork, the one he grabbed, might just serve. It consisted of a vise-grip locking pliers squeezing the wooden handle of a ball-peen hammer, the two united, forming a three-legged figure of substantial weight, with unsoldered, still detachable components.

Will sprinted to his dorm, and, weighted down a bit, nevertheless sprinted back to the crowd of students and staff facing down Admin. Will did an end run around to the front, leaped up onto a drain pipe, and stepped over to the window ledge neighboring it. Left hand on the pipe, right leg on the ledge, left leg dangling, his right hand was free to use the tools in his suspended pants and pants pocket

His long, thin frame had made him the rope-climbing star of any gym class. His reach brought him 8" closer to the top than his shortest peers, and no huge gluteus maximus weighed him down. Gluteus minimus, if anything. Climbing came naturally to him.

But climbing, breaking and entering pseudo-gothic structures was another story, especially with no nubbbins or gargoyles to grab onto, and tempered, double-glazed, 12 over 12 windows, some ogival, to be penetrated.

As he raised the hammer for the first thunderous strike, he was grabbed by his hanging leg, and pulled off the wall into the muscular arms of John Hemings, Bella's Capt'n father.

"My daughter is one of the students in there, and I don't want her surrounded by any violence."

"Who is that?" Will asked, alerted by the color of the hands that held him. What a way to meet a possible father-in-law.

"I want to marry your daughter."

Hysterical laughter.

The Hemings power couple talked down the crowd, and in only two phone calls from a nearby booth, summoned Fieldstone's top administrators, and from them, appealing to their nobility and progressive politics, obtained a written and signed document to be demonstrated through the window to the protesting students agreeing to each of their demands — after which they burst hungrily through the front door, and headed to the dining hall for their first food in 18 hours.

Sitting at a table with Bella, they beckoned over, and introduced Will, her would-be savior, bashfully sitting two tables away.

"I know him," Bella said. "He asked me to the prom."

"Aren't you going to thank him?"

"For what? He didn't do anything."

"I stopped him from breaking into the building, the Captain said.

"Big deal," was her reply, and she walked away to confer with her comrades.

Will's tools were plopped on the table à trois, and became an obvious excuse for discussion.

"Nice hammer you've got there," Captain Hemings observed. "Not everyone has one of those ball-peens."

"I've got a lot of tools," Will said. "I collect them."

"Why is that?" Mrs. Hemings asked.

"I just like them. The ones I bring to school, sometimes I make sculptures out of them for art class. These were once a sculpture."

"What do you mean?" Mrs. Hemings most curious.

Will fastened the vice-grip toward the top of the hammer handle, adjusted the angles, and set the triangular structure down on the table.

"I call it 'Isolde Cinches Tristan for the Prom'. See, these are her legs under her ball dress, and here he's holding back, resisting, but she's got hold of his...um, leg."

"Would you sell this piece to us?" the Mrs. asked. "Just as a souvenir of this night?"

"Well, I guess, sure. I could always make one again."

"How much would you ask?"

"The hammer was about four dollars, and the pliers, maybe three fifty...plus tax...so say eight dollars?"

"But this is an artwork, not just the pieces it's made of. You should be asking artwork prices. For your inspiration."

"And genius."

"I don't know about genius. I mean it's pretty obvious."

"How many sculptures like this do you think there are in the world?"

"Um…none, maybe. One, two? What do you think would be an artwork price?"

"Would you take $700 dollars?"

"Isolde Cinches Tristan" would be the centerpiece, along with its story, at Chez Katrine's next show, then be permanently mounted atop the instrument panel of the *Atlantis*, often leered or chuckled at by its various crews.

I don't know the financial endpoint of this particular deal. (After all, three-figure sums were commonplace in the Vanderbilt household.) I do know that it began a series of constructive projects for Fieldstone upper: a summer oceanographic semester, crewing aboard the *Atlantis*, and ad libitum work-study in *haute-couture* chez Chez Katrine on W. 14th in the city.

Will was impressed for the first *Atlantis* summer crew, largely by order of Bella, who wanted to keep him out of her hair. But being with her father on a tight ship did not aid Will's forgetting, and with disembarquement the problem remained: Will a third year Upper, wanting to take Bella, now a first year Upper, to his graduation prom — a setup for the denouement, or perhaps de-denouement, and in any case, the crux of the story.

To wit:

"If you won't go out with me, I'll kill myself." the Grand Intimidator figured. "That's got to work. She'll give me a kiss at the end, right?

Bella and Will were walking in different directions along the quad, when, after a night of inner-struggle and lucubrations, Will was determined to pop the question. As he came within a yard of her, he stopped, and said, "Bella?". Much practiced in cynical politeness, she too stopped, and said, "Will?"

"I'd like to take you to the prom."

"Now why would I want that?"

"Because if you don't, I'll kill myself."

"So?"

"So you'll be to blame for my death."

"So?"

"So you'll have my death on your conscience."

"You don't know my conscience."

"You think I'm kidding."

"I hope you're not."

This was not going as Will had planned.

"OK. This week. You'll see. See you."

"Not if I see you first."

The deed was done. The handkerchief was thrown. The face was slapped. Now he would have to go ahead with it. The first question was why did he like this perfectly awful girl, who wouldn't give him the time of day, and even wanted him dead? I pass.

But, next came the PLAN, the PRACTICE, and the PERFORMANCE.

There were the stages of death to consider:

1. slightly dead (decrepitude)
2. more dead (at death's door)
3. mostly dead (no vital signs)
4. very dead (buried and left)

#4 was out. Why, exactly, she should want to go to the prom with a disappeared corpse — he didn't get that far. The proximate trick was to pull off being as-it-were-dead, an uncommon use of the subjunctive.

The first observers would no doubt summon Ellie Pransky, the school nurse. Because it was hard to get to #3, his technique would have to evade her pulse-taking and stethoscopy. Even assuming a very healthy, supra-Olympic pulse rate of 30 beats/minute, one every two seconds, Nurse Ellie would have to listen for at least three seconds, to be sure of hearing a beat. Let's say six, assuming a skipped beat. So Will, for safety's sake, figured he'd have to work his heartbeat down to slower than one every ten seconds. Make it fifteen. Surely, if one didn't feel a pulse by fifteen seconds, one would assume catastrophe. Nurse Ellie might start CPR. Yes, he'd get to feel her lovely lips on his mouth, but could he stand the compressions? Unknown A. And what if her lips made his heart beat faster? Unknown B.

So the PLAN favored #2 — to almost die, to lie there, in Bella's known itinerary, as-it-were-dead, to be taken away, and to see if she'd change her mind.

He'd be carried away, probably in an ambulance. To where? Could he get away with this at some Emergency Room? Make it two beats a minute. But they'd hook him up to some cardiac monitor. This wasn't going to work. Before making an alternate plan, he'd better see if he could do it at all.

He had read about yogis being able to stop their hearts, and if *someone* could do that, so might he. Hence the next two weeks of twice daily experimental PRACTICE. Here's what he worked out (you may try this, unsupervised):

THE TECHNIQUE OF INDUCING HUMAN TORPOR

1. Man bun to stop energy in and out of head.

2. Lying supine, stretch out back, as far as possible.

3. Place L ankle over R.

4. Interlace L and R fingers, with L thumb on top.

5. Place hands on breastbone with R pinky at the lower end.

6. Close eyes.

7. Completely fill lungs.

8. Breathe slowly, moving only enough air as needed, keeping upper lungs filled.

SEMI-DEATH BY ENFORCED SYMMETRY

Did it work? Yes! Slowly lifting one hand to feel neck, and with eyes on a clock, he had gotten his heart rate down to one every 14 seconds. Enough for a beginner. Back to the PLAN.

Bella would discover him dead. So far, so good. But he'd have to avoid professional examination or monitoring. So with peeking enough to be sure of some effect, when she was well beyond him, he'd have to skedaddle. Where? Anywhere. Just not to be seen for several days, to be the subject of urgent speculation, and to have the incident headlined in *The Fieldston News*, the school paper.

Nothing left then but to try to gaslight her, get her guilt-tripped and crazed enough to sign something saying she'd go to the prom with him, if he ever came back to life. He'd need an accomplice.

This was ridiculous. No roads led to the prom. He'd just stay home and mope. At least he'd learned to play intermittently dead.

CAR

For his eighteenth birthday, and doubling as a graduation present, his parents presented him with an envelope, containing a gift card for "One (1) car." The family, themselves, had four: a silver Rolls-Royce Phantom for special occasions, a yellow Ferrari Spider for fun rides, and a white Volvo V40 for just toodling around. Plus the old, black, Paul Robeson Packard, bodyworked, and refinished, but treated more as a souvenir. But Will could have any car he wanted. He could park it in front of the Packard door. So what did he want?

This is a difficult problem. Rolls and Royce, and Volvo were boring, Enzo Ferrari was more interesting, but Will wanted a car different from his parents'. Henry Ford was an antisemite. Volks and Wagen and Porsche were Nazis. He didn't want a Dodge Taurus since he was an Aries. Then, inspiration struck: a Hudson, a classic, emerald green, 1951 Hudson Hornet. This was a truly superb choice for at least five different reasons:

As the Hornet's loyal companion, driver, and faithful valet, Kato Vanderbilt, he could use his tools!

A step-down Hudson is weird, groovy, far out, and badass.

It was thoroughly over-engineered in the Hudson tradition, over-designed and over-built

And it was one of the top ten of America's most collectible cars, one of the industry's all-time greats.

Last, but not least, it evoked the great mystery of Henry Hudson, the haunted, gelid, hyperborean

ghost of Henry Hudson, set adrift in 1611 by his
mutinous, cowardly crew for his insistence on further
exploring what is now, ironically, called Hudson
Bay. Disappeared at sea. Set free to die, perchance
to dream, perhaps to hoof it down to New York
City? Why else would the Hudson River be named
the Hudson River, the Hudson River Bridge, the
Henry Hudson Parkway? The ghost of the vanished
Henry Hudson blown south on the vagaries of the
jet stream, as far south and west as Hudson Park in
Long Beach, CA.

Yes, a goblin-green Hudson Hornet who-
needs-muscles? muscle car, specially outfitted with
a buzz generator with which Will could notify
early-morning neighborhoods that he was on
the lookout, protecting them from all manner of
méchantes. And, believe it or not, that car could
always (magically!) find a parking place, even in the
busiest neighborhoods at the busiest times of day in
Manhattan. Find your destination, turn the nearest
corner, and there it was, in the first third of the block
on your side. And if it ever broke down, there in the

glove compartment was a genuine Hudson Repair Manual, so he could maybe use his tools.

However, for his eighteenth birthday, there also came what would normally be a less welcome present — an envelope from the Selective Service ordering him to register within 30 days of his 18th birthday, and noting that failure to register is a felony punishable by a fine of up to $250,000 and/ or 5 years imprisonment. Very friendly. Serve your country. After an evening's discussion concerning his Vanderbilting his way out (Charles was good friends with the Secretary of the Navy), Will decided to go it on his own, using his own wits, against the dimwits of the military. His parents reluctantly agreed to stand behind him.

By March, 1967, the Vietnam War was no joke. President Johnson had half a million young people killing and dying (far more of the former than the latter) over there in a national effort to protect Liberty and Freedom throughout the world, though neither the logic nor the politics were completely clear. SDS was already two years into "teach-ins" which were being emulated on college campuses nationwide. Several Vietnamese monks, and an American, Norman Morrison, had burned themselves alive in protest, and Will's parents had taken him to the huge, June '65 rally at Madison Square Garden, where, amidst all-engulfing cheers, he heard Wayne Morse, Coretta King, and Benjamin Spock — he whose book had saved Will's foreskin — call for resistance to, and action against the war. Through old Cornell connections Charles and Gwen were friends of Spock's, and since he was still based in Cleveland, invited him to spend the night at their place — an offer he gratefully accepted, and was happy to appear the next morning at an impromptu assembly at the Fieldston School, where almost all of the audience had unknowingly been raised by him.

None had yet been selected by the Selective Service from the ritzy Fieldson School, though once anyone turned 18, the their fates (parental influence aside) were determined by the Deluxe Bingo Cage that spit out birthday dates contained in capsules.

Will got his notice in March of his senior year, another of his firsts at Fieldston. He had already made plans, and had registered with glee. By calling him, the Selective Service had fallen into his trap. He could now put his breathing techniques into practice without fear of subsequent chest compressions.

He would show up a day early, wearing a conservative suit, with white shirt and red, white, and blue striped tie. They would apologize to him for his mistake ("I'm sorry but, you'll have to come back…"), he would express his disappointment, he was so looking forward to this day, but they would be happy to see him tomorrow, as scheduled.

The Hudson found a parking place around the corner from the Selective Service office. At 10:00, fifteen minutes before his scheduled time, he was seen to fall face down across the entrance steps, looking every bit like one of those chalk outlines left on the street after the body has been removed. He was revived by a group of inductees behind him, helped up the stairs, and into the waiting room, where the incident was breathlessly reported by his helpers.

His pulse was checked by one of the examiners, who checked again at the carotid. While a normal resting pulse rate for someone his age might be 60-80 bpm, and an Olympic athlete's around 40-60, Will's was 32. His blood pressure was 82/38. The white-coated examiner was about to call an ambulance, but Will calmly explained that, for him, those were normal values. Yes, doctors couldn't explain it. They had recommended he eat plenty of red meat. But basically he was fine. "I'm fine, really fine, and I have no conscientious objection. I get these fainting spells every once in a while, but basically I'm fine. It's just a kind of heart condition..." His urine dip was normal.

He was not even asked to drop his drawers. He *was* asked about the Superman S sewn on to them.

"Oh, that's for Schopenhauer — I'm named after him. My parents were both philosophers at Cornell, along with Wittgenstein. Wittgenstein. That's who I'm named after."

The examiners were more non-plussed than annoyed, each in his own way. One, an amateur cellist, asked him about the music written in ball point pen on his hairless sternum.

"That's the famous Tristan Chord. You know, the unresolvable chord, sufficient unto itself, the way Tristan and Isolde are? Really, it's not that big a deal, only an augmented fourth, augmented sixth, and augmented ninth above any bass note you choose. I have an appointment for a permanent tattoo next week. So..."

"4F," a man at the table announced.

"4F? What does that mean?"

"It means we find you unfit for military service."

"You mean I can't join the army?" Getting angry. "You mean I'm not good enough for you?"

"Not every person's body can stand the rigors of training and combat, and we wouldn't want you to..."

"What? To get hurt? To get out of breath? I'm going to get my parents on this. They know the Secretary of the Navy."

"That will be enough, thank you. You'll receive your status card in the mail by next week. Next..."

"Next!" the attendant called out to the waiting room.

Having achieved his 4F, Will dressed, and walked down the stairs, still a little faint, but without falling. Et resurrexit.

Never having studied music, music theory, or even the piano (though they had a Steinway grand in the living room), Will had no idea what any of that augmented stuff meant. It sounded impressive. But in a neurotic preference for accuracy, he wanted to get it all correct, so sat down and memorized it. It wasn't entirely fraudulent, because he remembered being drawn in, whoosh, fixated, when he had first heard that sound at the Amato.

He was unsteady on his feet. These were dangerous games. This heart, breath and blood pressure business had consequences. Not necessarily when he practiced it, supine, in bed, but out in the real world, climbing steps, performing for people more powerful or consequential than he. The curve of descending vital signs was asymptotic, ever more closely approximating death. He would need to be sure that, given real-world stressors, it did not approach too closely. He would need to study more carefully the science and practice of resurrection.

PART TWO

Annapolis, Maryland, the state capitol, attracts many visitors with its charm. Old, brick-lined sidewalks, fresh seafood, historic architecture located along the banks of the Severn River heading for Chesapeake Bay. If one looks at a map, one sees two neighboring rectangular areas, corner to corner at King George St. and College Ave, nose to nose, mano a mano, the one, appropriately, a border of St. John's College, and the other bordering the United States Naval Academy, in whose history, much blood was shed, much flesh burnt, and much sea-water inhaled battling the very King George of the street signs. Each year, out of tens of thousands of applicants, each recommended by a senator or congressional representative, a thousand or so are selected by the Academy as plebes, first-year freshmen, en route via "The Yard" to becoming midshipmen officers of the US Navy.

Along the other street, as mentioned earlier, and appropriately calling up a severed head on a platter, lay "The College", the most contrarian of all US colleges, choosing to serve up platterfulls of only the greatest thoughts that have been thought, by the greatest minds that have pondered, now immortalized in books without cover graphics. Johnnies thought such books were, or would be, or should be given a chance to be, hot stuff, and good for them.

Over at The Yard, the few plebes or midshipmen who might have agreed that, say, the *Iliad* was hot, would have marked passages like

"When Meriones, giving chase, caught up with Phereclus, he lunged with his spear, and the point went in the right buttock, under the bone, and into the bladder beneath."

or

"Then mighty Diomedes, bringing his huge sword down on Hypeiron's collarbone, he sheared his shoulder clean off from the neck and back."

Taken together, nose to nose, the two rectangles made an odd-shaped yin and yang, with a scholarly yin dot in the would be martial yang, and a soldierly yang dot in the wannabe-learnèd yin.

Other, more subtle, similarities were also at play. For instance, both institutions each had one or more illicit meth labs among their dorm rooms, (that's meth as in methamphetamine), making meth from Sudafed. Why? At each school, there were many students with stuffy noses, and in each school, chemistry was part of the curriculum. And both schools' recruitment come-ons claimed its curriculum would make for success in later life, though St. John's reasoning was necessarily more serpentine.

A third reason was that while both curricula were so demanding, making meth from Sudafed was so easy! What's wrong with having something easy to do in life? Here, look at these molecular structures:

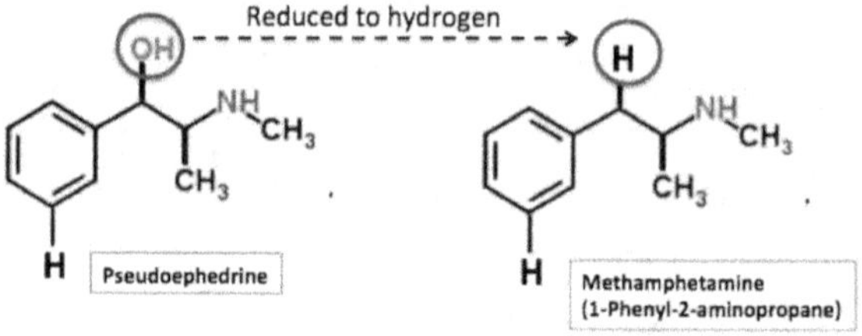

Take the O out of the OH, and you've got it —
a standard process called "chemical reduction."
There are several methods that can effect this
transformation, using reagents found or obtainable
by any organic chemistry lab, even at St. John's
College, and of course via the US Navy. Detailed
instructions for home- or dorm-room labs were
widely published, either in underground newspapers,
or mimeographed treasures like the early *Anarchist
Cookbook*, and many students, graduate and
undergrads, were walking around with stuffy noses,
exactly because of a local scarcity of decongestants.
Further, who can deny that meth might be of great
aid in studying a twelve-foot shelf of "the Great
Books", end to end?

Will's first glimpse of June was in May of 1967, when he visited St. John's for his requested admissions interview. He drove the Green Hornet non-stop for four hours, directly into the admissions parking lot, and walked into a small colonial house. The interview was a breeze. They had loved his admissions essay on "Emotional Eccentricity in *Tristan and Isolde* ", were amused by his Superman T-shirt, which an admissions officer had spotted through his new white shirt, and that what's more, he told them that the S was for Socrates, Spinoza, Schopenhauer, and Sartre, depending, *and* that he would be paying full tuition — so it was really he who was interviewing them. Will was finished — and accepted — by 4:30, was invited to have dinner in the dining hall, and, if he chose not to drive back in twilight and darkness, to stay the night in a dorm. At dinner, he noticed a poster on a bulletin board announcing a HERNDON MONUMENT CLIMB, open to the public, on the Naval Academy campus a couple of blocks away. He had actually spent the night wondering, even worrying about potential conflict between the heady, hippie Johnnies, and the who knows what, but far from heady and hippy, crew-cutted warrior neighbors.

So at 7:30 the next morning, he began the short walk over to the Naval Academy to see what he could see. What he saw were people streaming from several directions toward the main quad in front of the chapel. There stood a large obelisk, the center of attention, which, he imagined, must be the Herndon Monument. Who Herndon was, and what the monument celebrated, he did not know, but as he got nearer, he saw that the granite had been greased with something white, like Crisco, and at the bottom was scrawled PLEBES NO MORE! 5/17/67. The growing crowd contained uniformed student sailors, their likely parents around them, a few older Navy types, also in uniform, and various young working men and women, who may also have been students, and a number of miscellaneous, unattached civilians. Scattered among them, Will spied twenty or so strangely dressed characters, as if from another planet, entering his field of vision at least, perhaps choreographed and timed, in chronological order, walking in exaggeratedly slow pace, as if they were dancers moving in jello. Among them were

— a soldier from some ancient Greek war?

— a Don Quixote type, who must be very hot in that half-suit of armor

— someone who looked like pictures he'd seen of Mozart, or was it Beethoven?

— Huck Finn, no doubt

— a Valkyrie maiden with quite sharp horns

— a man in a whale costume, dragging its tail

— clearly Karl Marx

— a young woman in an Einstein wig (not very convincing, perhaps a feminist critique of patriarchal physics).

After a few minutes, Will realized they must all be spies, critics, satirists, or jesters from St. John's, a small cabal committed to keeping their Annapolis neighbors at a boiling point — those, at least, who had any idea of who the characters were, or what was their intention. Worse come to worst, the midshipmen knew they could overpower, and if necessary, kill them.

Herndon Climb is the rite of passage that enables the freshmen to escape the degrading cocoon of "plebedom", to emerge and spread their wings in the bright air of "fourth class midshipmen". That includes the oddly many young women who see the Navy as a liberating career. The "climb" is actually the building of a several hundred person human pyramid surrounding a 21-foot granite obelisk. 21 feet is high, but not that high — a little higher than a two story house with normal ceilings.

The objective of this climb is to remove from the pyramidal top of the monument, the "dixie cup cover" — the denigrating name for the headgear plebes have been previously assigned — which looks like a white "sailor's hat" of the popular imagination, with a blue stripe around its rim. The objective — to knock this insulting piece of headgear off the top (how it got there, no one but upperclassmen knew — probably via some extension-arm machine, brought silently in the middle of the night) — to knock that offending topper aside, and to replace it with a regulation midshipman's "cover", a black-peaked white hat with a blue band, and a Navy insignia prominent on the front, and celebrate the official end of the plebe year.

You would think that a class of almost a thousand would-be warriors would have no problem linking arms and body masses, being crawled upon by, and supporting somewhat lighter others, and this grouping being crawled upon again, the third layer acting as the foothill for the final climb, a culminating challenge reinforcing the moral, mental, and physical development they have been rigorously training since induction. And, yes, they wouldn't have had a problem — except that the obelisk had been greased against a climb with 250 pounds of Crisco, and the participants were continuously sprayed with cold water from an array of hoses.

(This huge quantity of Crisco was donated each year, at taxpayer expense, by Proctor &

Gamble, whose huge tax deduction was greased, administration after administration, by the appointed Secretary of the Navy.)

On Wednesday, May 17, 1967, at 800 hours sharp, a blast of sports whistles let loose a stampede of shirtless, muscle-built late-teenaged males, along with twenty-odd one-piece swimsuited strapping young women, charging toward the monument. Working together, they used their shirts to wipe the granite clean of Crisco, but those shirts also spread a thin film on the rock face, one equally slippery. After three hours plus of climbing and falling, climbing and wiping and falling, a tall, slim youngster, standing atop the sweating, linked-arm human pyramid below him, managed to whip the dixie cup "sailor hat" off with his shirt, and reaching high above himself, after multiple tries, to toss the white hat up onto the obelisk point so that it stayed. The crowd went wild. "O! O! O! O!" they chanted. Wrapping one arm around the pillar, O called out into the din, "God bless America! God bless the Naval Academy!" and with his free hand, he waved to someone particular in the crowd. Will thought he located the waver's object, a lovely, long-haired, waif-like figure, garbed in high hippie style. But when the winner jumped down onto the heap of no-longer-plebes, and from there to the ground, the crowd began to mill around, and Will lost sight of the girl-woman. But not before he was already in love. Et resurrexit.

O. North of San Antonio, Texas — now Midshipman O. North — was the 20-year-old hero who had finally placed the upperclassman's hat on top of the monument. Ashamed of his faggy birth name, he went by "O. as in O. Henry" among the literate, and "as in O.J. Simpson" among the jocks. His family was there to congratulate him on the accomplishment. "I couldn't have done it without them — all of them!" he exclaimed, sweeping his long arm toward his teammates, and across the crowd. Then he and his parents charged off to find the girl he had written and talked about, but she had disappeared.

Where was she? Slightly late for her job at the

Sunoco station just north of campus, where Will
stopped to fill the Hornet up before heading out
of town.

Fortuitous? Too fortuitous? Author tilting
the pinball machine? Sorry, these things happen,
no doubt antecedent to every significant surprise
encounter. Earlier, only glimpsed and imagined, and
now, there she was in overalls, actually asking, one to
one, "What can I do for you?"

The revolutionary sixties were also a
revolutionary time for gas stations, balancing the
cost of attendants with the cost of installing new
pumps which would allow self-service, with the
cost of runaway drivers scooting off after filling
up, with the cost of cameras to capture the license
plates of such drivers, with the cost of insurance,
should customers splash their clothing or their eyes
with gas, or step in gas puddles from over-filled
tanks and ruin their shoes. In 1967, Maryland was
mixed for self-service, and Earl's Sunoco was still
"full-service" with attendants who would pump gas,
wash windows, wipe headlights, check radiators,

give directions, hand out maps, and if asked, check and fill radiators and batteries with water, tires with air, and not expect a tip. Earl felt he was being a good citizen, employing generations of townies in a small city whose teen employment was otherwise monopolized by the College, and the Navy.

Will needed only gas, but, seeing his New York plates, his attendant (was it *she*??) asked if he was headed out of town, and hearing that he was, recited the litany of services she had been trained to offer. On this southern afternoon in May, she wore no typical gas station cover-all, but her own overalls over a t-shirt. And the bib of those overalls was quite the work of art. On it, someone, most likely she, had stitched her name, June, and around that name had embroidered a glorious landscape worthy of some anonymous Flemish embroiderer of the sixteenth century, anonymous because of gender. But in the world of art, all Will could think of was "June is bustin' out all over," which this slender young woman decidedly wasn't. Had she been, he would have been (silenced and) embarrassed, especially when, "buds bustin' out of bushes" move the song south in Will's imagination, and he turned back to stare at his dashboard, with the needle on the fuel gage slowly moving from E to F.

But he had already noticed June's fineness of limb and feature, her slanting partridge eyes, her dancer's bearing and grace. To his Wagner-tutored imagination, she seemed some combination of divine maiden and little witch, a head-turning mix of tomboy and sylph. How could he get her to talk to him, to interrupt her mechanical "full-service" routine? He was decidedly not a pick-up artist. Hence:

"Your name is June?"

"Yeah. So?"

"That's nice sewing on your overalls."

"I know."

"Do that yourself?"

"Yeah. Can I get you anything else?"

It was not as if there were other customers waiting.

"You from around here?"

"Yup."

"I'm from New York. From the City."

"You, like, applying to the College? You're like not the Academy type."

"How's that?"

"Well, first of all, they wouldn't take you. You're like too skinny. You'd never like last a week in training."

Will imagined he wouldn't do well at the bottom of the Herndon climb. But he thought he might be useful at the top. Lightweight. Long reach.

And during that imagined difficulty, there flashed into Will's mind an evening long past when Richard Dyer-Bennet, the great Scottish folk singer, an old Eton buddy of his father's, had stayed at the Mt. Kisco house after a concert at Town Hall. As is regrettably normal for such guests, he was asked by his hosts to sing a late-night song. This is what he sang:

The Laird of Cockpen, he's proud and he's great,
And his mind's taken up with the things of the state.
He wanted a wife, his proud house to keep,

Perhaps it was the iffy end-rhyme that had pasted the moment into Will's memory, but now it was the warning about wooin' that took center stage. Forewarned, but thus forearmed, he pressed ahead:

"How do you know so much about the Academy? Boyfriend?"

This last was daring.

"My Daddy works at the Yard, the Academy."

"What's he do? Wait, let me guess. Buildings and Grounds? (She stared at him.) Custodial? "

She laughed. More like sniggered.

"No. Yeah...sort of. He like cleans up a lot of stuff."

"Janitorial?"

"He's Dean of like Academic Studies. Admiral Dean Matthew Elder. Also teaches weaponry and submarines."

"Is he really an admiral?"

"I dunno. Maybe."

That should have been enough for anyone —

140

except Will.

"Would he let you go out with a St. John's student? I mean just in general. I'm not trying to be nosy, just to figure the sociology of the place."

"He probably like wouldn't like that. Besides, I already like have a boyfriend. But Daddy wouldn't tell me what to do. As he says, I'm not in his Navy."

"Is your boyfriend in his Navy?"

"You bet. Pick of the third year crop. Midshipman North, bright as the north star. Like personally selected and suggested for me by the Admiral."

"Your mom like him?"

"Mom's dead. Naval accident. I'm all Pop's got."

"You call him 'Pop'?"

"I call him like a lot of things. He likes 'Daddy'. Sometimes 'Daddy Superior', sometimes 'Pater Seraphicus'. Sometimes 'Bishop'. A couple times he like wanted 'Daddy Pope.'"

"Catholic, huh?"

"Up the gazoo."

"What's a gazoo?"

"Like where the sun don't shine."

"Ah, I see." (He didn't.)

She stood, and faced him, cross-armed, head cocked, challenging.

"Well. Nice meeting you," Will said. "See you end of summer when school starts."

"Not if I see you first."

Where had he heard *that* before? He drove off northward, pondering.

If this was the beginning of something, it was off to a poor start.

Over the summer, they wrote to one another, or rather Will wrote to June (c/o Earl's Sunoco) and waited, in vain, for a response. During that summer, U.S. troops in Vietnam increased to 300 thousand, and huge protests were held in Washington, D.C., New York City and San Francisco. Will attended none of them, concerned that if something happened to him, he might miss a letter from June, or be postponed in responding.

At the end of August, the Green Hornet, with Will at the wheel, drove south for what would be their last time. Will stopped at Earl's Sunoco on the way in to Annapolis, but June was not there — for which he was relieved, and secretly grateful.

St. John's College

Here is what Will had ahead of him in his first, and last, Johnnie year. Column A, he confidently expected; Column B, he had read about in the College literature, and Column C, he was kind-of-sort-of aware of as it was happening, though it must be said that neither he, nor the Great Books were all that interested. For the latter, it was "So what else is new?"

A	B	C
SEPTEMBER 1967	Homer *Iliad, Odyssey,* Aeschylus *Agamemnon, Libation Bearers, Eumenides.*	Nguyen Van Thieu wins the presidential election of South Vietnam under a newly enacted constitution.

OCTOBER 1967	Herodotus *Histories* Plato *Gorgias, Protagoras. Meno,* Sophocles *Antigone.*	U.S. Secretary of State Dean Rusk states that proposals by the U.S. Congress for peace initiatives are futile, because of North Vietnam's opposition.
NOVEMBER 1967	Plato *Republic, Apology, Crito, Aristophanes Clouds.*	In the Battle of Dak To, U.S. forces resist an offensive by communist forces, and suffer 1,800 casualties.
DECEMBER 1967	Plato *Phaedo, Theaetetus,* Sophocles *Oedipus Rex,* Aeschylus *Prometheus Bound.*	Benjamin Spock and Allen Ginsberg are arrested for protesting against the Vietnam War. The Summer of Love is held in San Francisco.
JANUARY 1968	Thucydides *Peloponnesian War.*	North Vietnamese communists launch the Tet Offensive. The assault contradicts the Johnson administration's claims that the communist forces are weak and the U.S.-backed south is winning the war.

FEBRUARY 1968	Plato *Symposium* *Aristotle Nicomachean Ethics.*	Feb 11-17 records 543 American deaths ,the highest number of the war. South Carolina State campus: police open fire on students protesting segregation. Three protesters die and 27 more are wounded.
MARCH 1968	Aristotle *Politics*, Lucretius *On the Nature of Things.*	Mar 16 U.S. massacre at My Lai, more than 500 civilians are murdered by U.S. forces. LBJ halts bombing north of the 20th parallel. Facing backlash about the war, he announces he will not run for re-election.
APRIL 1968	Aristotle *Physics.*	Martin Luther King Jr. is fatally shot on the balcony of the Lorraine Motel. Over the next week, riots in more than 100 cities nationwide leave 39 people dead, more than 2,600 injured and 21,000 arrested.

MAY 1968	Euripides *Bacchae, Medea,* Sophocles *Oedipus at Colonus , Ajax, Philoctetes,* Aristotle *Poetics*	Nine antiwar activists enter a Selective Service office in Catonsville, Maryland, remove nearly 400 files and burn them in the parking lot with homemade napalm. spurring some 300 similar raids on draft boards over the next four years. The Supreme Court rules 7-1 that burning a draft card is not an act of free speech protected by the First Amendment.
JUNE 1968		Robert F. Kennedy wins the California presidential primary—and is assassinated at the Ambassador Hotel in Los Angeles.
JULY 1968		LBJ signs the Treaty on the Non-Proliferation of Nuclear Weapons. Pope Paul VI reaffirmS the Roman Catholic Church's opposition to artificial contraception.

AUGUST 1968		The Soviet Union invades Czechoslovakia. At the Democratic National Convention in Chicago, police and National Guards rampage, clubbing and tear-gassing hundreds of antiwar demonstrators, news reporters and bystanders.

Though always on his mind, June emerged again, as was no doubt appropriate, during Will's late September study of the *Eumenides*, Aeschylus's tale of the deities of vengance, the so-called "Kindly Ones". Winged beings they, with black robes, serpents twisting in their hair, and blood dripping from their eyes. Vengeance for what? In Oreste's case, for killing his mother to avenge her murder of his father. Dysfunctional family? It's more complex than that, and as Tolstoy says, "Every unhappy family is unhappy in its own way."

But in re Will, vengeance for what? He had not yet impacted the less-than-placid pool of her life. Perhaps vengeance in advance, for asking her other than for gas, and engaging in a bit of customer conversation briefly touching on a cartoon character named Freddy the Flea who could jump over walls.

Or maybe a pursuing a Furies theme simply evolved from this: On September 25, Will found a flea on his pillow. He had never seen a flea before. Mrs. Mellert's bunny did not have fleas, nor did his family, nor the dropped cat. But after seeing it jump many times its height, and after further inspection with the lens on his Swiss Army super-knife, "flea" was his first hypothesis, and likely correct. It looked like the photo of a flea in the Greenfield Library's *Britannica.*

But June had not come into his dorm room leaving a flea or fleas behind. She did, however, note the ad he had placed in the Capital Gazette: WANTED: fleas for class experiment. Contact Will Vanderbilt at SJC. (It was exactly 10 words, $1.50). Will had cleverly thought to entrap a possible responder.

Given the general, off-beat cleverness of the
Johnnies, June's curiosity had been piqued, and
after a week or so, June cold-called him to ask what
was going on, flea-wise. Thinking he had her, he
answered, "Come over, and I'll show you," His S that
day was for Sneaky, or even Sivana.

You can't blame June for imagining a full-blown
flea circus. Flea-orchestras have played audible
music for frock-coated and gowned flea dancers
in great flea ballrooms. And the documentary had
featured an exposition of training tactics, from the
lowest slavery of fleas glued or wired to the seats of
miniature machines, to the latest, most sophisticated
conditioning of flea belief systems resulting in happy
fleas performing antics for their happy flea-trainers.
She'd seen it on TV. Fleas tight-rope walking, diving
from a high board into a saucer of water, jumping
through flaming hoops, and riding, bareback, on
small white mice. Perhaps Will Vanderbilt at SJC —
whoever he was — might have that and more to show.

"It's you," she said, when they met up on the
Library steps at the end of September.

"It's you," he said, more flabbergasted than she.

"I came about the fleas."

He had been expecting some upper-class Johnnie.

"What fleas?"

"For the class experiment."

In spite of the word-counting and ridiculous fee, he...

He laughed, and moved in to give her a hug.

She laid him on the floor, gasping, with a right to the solar plexus. Navy karate class for Academy staff kids.

So began a closer friendship, she in embarrassment, he in awe and fear. For many reasons, mostly invented, like topping off, or window washing, the Green Hornet was often seen at Earl's Sunoco. For her birthday, Will had given her a Fred & Ginger, components newly purchased at Annapolis Hardware, now extra-decorated with cornsilk hair, and acrylic tux and gown. For his, she responded with a Great Book, whose cut-out compartment, usually dedicated to marijuana, was filled with lead shot. DO NOT DROP, it said on the cover, and even early on it was unclear whether the implied command referred to the book, or to her.

But for all the jokey playfulness, the affair was necessarily cloaked — heavily — in secrecy, a hard-to-come-by quality in the small community of intellectual searchers and weirdos. June was never seen at Waltz nights or contra dances — but then, neither was Will. June did leave notes, some in treasure-hunt fashion, indicating where the next note was to be found.

How did she command the interstices of the St. John's campus? Her invisibility consisted of an old blue-striped suit, and an Einstein-y wig, in remarkable imitation of some of the old Europeans that often showed up as guest speakers for Friday Night Lectures, which, free and open to the public, she could attend undisguised, though always in unrevealing, older-woman clothing, varied enough to avoid being an identified, to-be-wondered-about "presence" on campus. Hiding is fun, especially in public spaces. Daddy didn't mind her attending the lectures, as long as she occasionally attended some of the Academy's own.

Her last note to Will, the end of a treasure hunt, read as follows:

Let everything happen:
Beauty and terror, ever onward,
No effort is final.

Nearby is the country they call life.
You will know it by its seriousness.
Give me your hand.

What was *that*? Did she write it? Was it Rilke?

And what of Midshipman North — he who had displaced the dixie cup hat from the Herndon monument, and then waved to Junie before jumping down?

"Oh, don't worry about Ollie. He doesn't know anything about us, or what I do weekdays when I'm not at work. They keep them plenty busy in the Yard."

This system, playfully touch and go, began to break down at the annual Croquet match in mid-April, the month of Aristotle's *Physics*, and the battle of Khe Sanh, the month when thousands of Vietnamese civilians were killed by the US, some via naval bombing, the month when Martin Luther King was shot, and tens of thousands of Americans were arrested in domestic rioting.

THE ANNAPOLIS CUP

And in this world condition, both St. John's College, and the US Naval Academy thought it important to demonstrate civilian/military amity in a symbolically subtle, and exceptionally odd, annual event, a game of lawn croquet.

The first thing to be admitted, is that croquet is a sissy sport. There is no physical contact, no endurance is required, and it calls forth not a drop of sweat greater than demanded by normal perspiration under local conditions. So why would a macho military choose to take part? As wags of the time would say, "Join the Navy; travel to exotic, distant lands; meet exciting, unusual people, and kill them." What happened to that? It is irrelevant that one can easily kill someone with a croquet mallet. Never in recorded history had this been recorded.

It must be noted, too, that NA midshipmen were not just potential killer-grunts, but their future leaders, currently being groomed. Many of their parents and grandparents were of a class to request and receive nominations from Congressmen and Senators, and even from the Vice President of the United States.

The midshipman croquet team, though only two groups of three, marched from the Academy, down College Ave, backed up by some thirty wind, brass and percussion players from the Navy Marching band, blaring such old favorites as *Anchors Away, The American Sailor, Brave Souls,* and *The Armed Forces on Parade,* all, of course, in a strongly marked 4/4 time, maintaining their tradition of musical excellence and professionalism, all in their dress blues, white gloves and hats, led by a drum major with be-badgèd sash, and foot-and-a-half high bearskin "cap", towering over him like a hairy, threatening thought-form, marking out the beat with an enormous, potentially murderous, staff, in step, rigid, brilliantly performing MUSIC that has never known a pianissimo. To save their embouchures, they occasionally broke into a cadence count, one, two, three, four, and once through the St. John's gate, brought forth their acerbic verse,

> *We are great big, ugh, hairy, hairy men!*
> *We know where we are goin'*
> *and we know where we have been!*

which, considering the long-hairs they were taunting, and the long-hairs' oceanic scope of study, lost some of its punch — at least among the long-hairs and their long-haired studious consorts.

The middies lined up on their side of the playing field, accompanied by their mascot, "Bill the Goat", a costumed midshipman, sweating under a huge mask that might at one time been that of a pig, but which, updated with horns curled around its ears, now did passable service as a mountain goat. Why the Navy mascot was not more nautical is perhaps related to the sailor's perpetual fear of drowning.

What would the St. Johnnie's team, band, mascot, and groupies be wearing in response? Would they dress as nerds? No! Once the Navy band had reached its final double bar, out from every corner, from behind every bush, sprang The Fighting Axolotls of St. John's College. Pretty cool mascot, eh?

For those unacquainted:

The footish-long axolotl honored the Aztec god of fire and lightning, Xolotl, who had once disguised himself as a salamander to avoid being sacrificed. Fiery gills extended from either side of its neck. Not something you or I would have thought of. It has yet another superpower: if mortally wounded or even decapitated, it can regenerate limbs, lungs, heart, jaws, spines, and even parts of its brain from what's left! Every tissue can be replaced: skin, bone, cartilage, muscle, even stem cells. Organs can regenerate countless times and be completely functional. Had JFK been an axolotl,

there might never have been a Vietnam war for
students to protest.

Consequently, having no need of them — and
this was a biggie for the Johnnies — axolotls had
no sharp teeth or claws — thus emblemizing the
unique, civilizing mission of a College with as
much contempt for campus sports as for political
correctness. (At the time, the school actually owned
two axolotls, each kept by the official student axolotl-
keeper in its own fishtank in the biology wing of
McDowell, each eyeing the other with suspicion,
with satisfaction? with lust? Hard to tell.) The other,
secondary unofficial College mascot was of course
the platypus. But the College owned no platypi.

Back to the Johnny crowd: How do you embody
and express your mascot? How do you dress and
behave like an axolotl? You don't. You dress oppositely,
covering the body with the oddest and most colorful
assortment of hats, blouses, skirts, dresses, pants short
and long, shoes of all kinds, and colorful socks, such
as no axolotl — short of those at the College — had
ever seen. And you behave with most unaxolotlish

abandon, jumping around and screaming expletives in Middle English, Latin, and Greek.

For some inexplicable reason, the Johnnies were the undisputed champs of the croquet world. They had beaten Navy in five out of every six games. Consequently, annually, and from the Navy's point of view, they had to be taken down. If for this, and no other reason, the gaiety of the day was seasoned with high tension. But within this soup, there was a smaller, sharper ingrediential strain.

I have spoken above about June's playful games of hide-and-go-seek on the College campus. For this Annapolis Cup, she continued her satire of the "great books" dressed as Oliver Twist's mother, wretched, bedraggled, and hugely pregnant, staggering her way to a workhouse. What, Will wondered, was her message to him in this? That she was somehow his mother, that the College was a workhouse for the intellectually rich, i.e. the imprisoned poor? But who else should she have come as, Mrs. Bumble?

He, enmeshed in seminars, had come as a snake-haired Eumenis. Why not? Besides, he wanted to try fashioning the snakes. He'd considered Slinkies, but they were too fat. He'd have room for only one or two, and they'd look like overweight antennae. He found a skinny spring in the Baltimore Specialty Store, the mechanism for springing a Jack-in-the-box. You turned the handle, and prongs were picked to play "I Love You Truly". In the empty measure after the listener being assured by "truly, dear," a small skeleton jumped out toward the grinder's face. Now this, Will thought, was real genius. A lesser mind might have had a snake or a frog spring out, but how often do snakes or frogs jump in peoples' faces? On the other hand, how often does death? Only $1.59 plus tax to be reminded of one's mortality? Cheap at half the price.

Cost being no issue to a Vanderbilt, he bought the last five in the store, and fastened the springs in the shape of the Pentagon onto a mortarboard from Annapolis Bridal and Tuxedo. From a back room, he also rented a whole-body bunny costume, as some kind of distorted remorse for the intended bunnicide in Mrs. Mellert's class so long ago.

Such was Will's version of going on a protest
march: the Eumenides shimmying away atop a white
rabbit, whose impromptu choreography would have
been a wonder to the Prince of Darkness himself.
It was a great hit with Will's fellow Johnnies, all so
recently poisoned by Aeschylus. Dancing skeletons
atop an Easter bunny, Death as the topping of a
cuddly life. So "meaningful" to the approving crop
of ancient teenage scholars. Though it must be said
that their understanding of "the Easter bunny" did
not even approach in complexity the occult, chimeric
origins of his royal furriness.

(To wit: The Passover Bunny arose — inevitably
— from his parent's mixed marriage:

— A PB&J sandwich had always indicated the
inter-mushing of the Passover Bunny and Jesus.

— An empty seat with full place setting was
always left for PB at the Seder table. His wine glass,
always full at the start of the meal, diminished little
by little with each sip prescribed in the ritual. No
one was ever caught sipping, though trying to catch
the culprit became as much part of the ceremony

as rejoicing in the punishments of the Egyptians.
No matter what family was invited to share in the
sumptuous setting, no one would fess up to the deed.
The glass was drained in four successive sips. *Blessed
art Thou, Lord our God, King of the Universe, who has
created the fruit of the vine.*

"But who was drinking the wine?"

"The Passover Bunny."

"And Jesus?"

"No."

"Why can no one see him?"

"Because he's magic."

"Did the Passover Bunny give the ten plagues to
the Egyptians?"

"No."

"Like spread them?"

"No."

"A few of them? Lice, plague, boils?"

"No."

"Any of them?"

"I don't know."

"Did he kill all the firstborn?"

"No."

"Did he kill Jesus?"

"No."

"Am I a firstborn?"

"Yes."

These were far more than "The Four Questions". Not to mention:

"Did they have Dr. Bronners then?"

"No. You know I went out with him...."

Whatever that meant. He didn't ask about Semmelweis.

But somehow, the killing of the first born always brought up for him — from childhood unto death — his attempt at killing Miss Mellert's bunny with *poisson*, halted in midstream, as with Abraham and Isaac, though without angelic intervention.)

SPORT

By avoiding demonstrations, what he unfortunately missed, three months into his first semester, and only just down the road, was The Levitation of the

Pentagon, that figure inscribed on his croquet hat, all
two billion pounds of it. He was just "too busy", an
excuse he regretted for the rest of his life.

On October 21, 1967 the National Mobilization
Committee to End the War in Vietnam called
for a mass rally at the Lincoln Memorial, offering
a concert by Phil Ochs. Norman Mailer, Robert
Lowell, Dwight MacDonald, Noam Chomsky,
and Paul Goodman, among more than a hundred
thousand others were there to listen to the music and
speeches by Dave Dellinger and Dr. Spock.

From there, half the protesters marched on
to the Pentagon — only to be met by soldiers
of the 82nd Airborne who formed a barricade,
bayonets-mounted, blocking the Pentagon steps.
Abbie Hoffman vowed to levitate the Pentagon
with psychic energy, and, with the help of Allen
Ginsberg's Tibetan chants, cause it to turn orange
and begin to vibrate, all of which energy would end
the War. When some protesters tried to get inside
the building, tear gas and rifle butts were used to
push back the crowd. Protesters faced bayonets,

put flowers in rifle barrels, and tried to chat with a taciturn front line of soldiers, until at midnight, most left to get some sleep as the troops kept guard.

He could have been there. He should have been there. And now, half a year later, dressed as a bunny with furies swaying on his head, he was dancing, hippity-hop, facing a sea of sailors with pentagonish malevolent intent. Similar, but not the same. Possibly worse.

Who was there, too, was Midshipman North — he who had displaced the dixie cup hat from the Herndon monument, had placed it on Junie's head, and was now standing at attention, cornet in hand, facing the Johnnie weirdness-array assembling haphazardly across the lawn.

"Oh, don't worry about him," June had said. "He doesn't know anything about us, or what I do weekdays when I'm not at work."

But that was then, and this was now. While Aristotle's *Physics* had remained constant, the same could not be said about MSM North, or the eyes he was bringing to the croquet match in front of him. Those eyes were not entirely his own, for he had alerted the members of his Intelligence and National Security class to the security issue being played out in front of them: the kidnapping by the enemy of a high-valued member of their community. Consequently, when she appeared on the Johnnie side of the lawn, pregnant, often relating to an oddly-topped rabbit (you know, like effing-like-bunnies), the stratagem was settled, and June and Will were centered in USNA spyglasses for much of the game. Every move, no matter what — the merest gesture — could be interpreted as proof positive of the condemning hypothesis, and by the end of the afternoon, suppressed rage was the dominant emotion of the midshipmen, if not among their visiting parents and friends.

Suppressed rage was merely a topper on routinely suppressed anger. While the average IQ of the midshipmen was lower than that of the Johnnies, it was not so low as to be unaware of the implied criticism, even scorn, in the contrast between their in-step-four-abreast order, and the clearly mocking anarchy of the Great Books crew. Who would want those namby-pambs defending the nation in time of war? What would they do — throw ideas at the enemy? But naval and national dignity must be maintained, though they could crush the Johnnies at will, like roaches.

The Johnnies, too, were quite aware of the underlying struggle. Because they couldn't afford to go mano a mano with the brutes, they restricted their derision to what they thought of as either sub- or supra-naval intelligence level. For instance, no group of four abreast would ever form among them, and no music in 4/4 would be played, lest it be heard as praise for the Pride of the Yard, the Navy's well-trained marching band. What would go over or under the heads of whom was never confirmed, because it was never tested. But the general scenario held.

St. John's, of course, had its own intelligence gathering operation — The Great Spooks Program — which used the Hearndon Climb and Annapolis Cup

as two large petri dishes during which the behavior
of the Other could be observed. Will had early been
recruited to the GSP on account of his well-noticed
habits of sneaking around, the obfuscations and
disappearances related to his clandestine activities
with "that girl", his "princess Nausicaa", servant,
no doubt, of the goddess Athena. And he had
recruited his seminar mates to train their often-thick
eyeglasses on the men in blue, their families, and most
potentially dangerous, their unshepherded friends.
After the match, the Great Spooks would gather at
dinner to discuss and debate what they had learned, as
the GSP Secretary took notes.

What had they learned from this match of April
17, 1968? Maybe it was only a surreptitious sadness
or glee at the death of Martin Luther King only
two weeks earlier, but it seemed to the GSP that the
Navy Band fortes were a little louder, their accents
somewhat sharper, more aggressive, and their meter
more machine-like, with fewer rubatos and shorter
fermatas. And that was only the music. The Band
stared directly at them as they played, and so too did

the Band groupies, and even the Band's sweeties, their "chicks". Instead of the normal milling-around of a crowd, the warrior group across the lawn seemed focused, platoon-like, all drilling their eyes into their bookish opponents. It didn't help that, as usual, the Johnnies beat the Navy 17-15, and 26-12. Good thing the Navy would not be defending the country with croquet mallets.

It was this day that Will was hit in the shoulder by a croquet ball that must have been launched by a golf swing, not the careful between-the-legs tap. But from who, from where? Why would whoever it was target *him*, hippity-hopping among the crowd? Probably just an accident. But what if it wasn't?

As the Band began its march back to the Academy, Cornettist Midshipman North ran over to Will, kneeled at his bare Eumenides feet, opened the spit valve on his horn, and let it drool on Will's right instep and between his toes while Will watched in wonderment. Then he grabbed June's hand, and with the other raised his midshipman's hat and put it on her head, saying to Will, "trim your sheets, lubber" and marched June away, back to the side she belonged to. Wiping his foot against his left calf, and scrubbing grass between his toes, Will found the spit to be of very low pH, reddening the skin, and causing intense burning. The cornettist ran to catch up with his band, dragging June behind him. The band was playing *Someday Over the Rainbow* to buoy themselves up, post-defeat.

And then, its Navy anthem, *Anchors Aweigh*. After two instrumental renditions, the band broke into singing:

Stand Navy down the field, sails set to the sky.
We'll never change our course, so Army you steer shy-y-y-y.
Roll up the score, Navy, Anchors Aweigh.
Sail Navy down the field and sink the Army, sink the Army Grey.

To the band, this made sense. To the naval families, this made sense. To the curious, neutral

spectator, this was confusing. To the assembled
Johnnies, ridiculous.

Sink the army? There was no army, except the
army of crazy Johnnies, who wouldn't go anywhere
near a recruiting booth. And the army "grey'? Lee's
confederate army, the Army of Northern Virginia
who weren't fighting naval battles? Exactly who were
we supposed to be rooting for? Well, what did words
matter, anyway? They were only words. Less than
words. Lyrics.

The front lawn cleared slowly, and Will was left
alone.

LOSING AN ONLY CHILD TO COLLEGE

As were Charles and Gwen, waving goodbye
to their only son, he, dressed like a bunny — a
Passover White Rabbit yet — with the added
attraction of skeletons on top, dancing wildly with
their staider partner bunny ears. Would the great
books be protectors of their child, or some demonic
hodgepodge of angelic advisers, each contradicting

another, and giving rise to a new manifestation of their son, their darling madman, and heir to the Vanderbilt name and fortune?

Which, for each, recalled their own version of being sat down for "the talk".

For Charles, it had meant instruction in the basics of the "class struggle", with the astonishing warning that — in spite of all that he could see, or had been told — the world in general, the world beyond his world, would consider him and his family, and his family's friends — all those who had always sent him birthday presents — "the bad guys". Probably his playgroup, too. Bad playgroup. How's that for a heritage and inheritance — being representative of Satan on earth?

For Gwen, the talk had been more complex, if possible. First, it involved being a girl among boys, then a young woman among young men, and for her high-school graduation, was accompanied by a late-war GI-pak of prophylactics. Her version for her son was simpler. "Don't get anyone pregnant, ok?"

A second layer of the Gwen "talk": instruction

in being a Jew in the post-war world, and earlier, being a Jew at all. The latter talk, of course, involved Hitler, and the practice of antisemitism, including the resentment of Jews for having "gotten us into" or even "caused" the war, the reason-beyond-reason for the death of their sons, and cause for further hatred.

But that part was easier than the pre-war part of "the talk" to a younger girl, the "being a Jew at all talk". How's that for a heritage and inheritance at the end of the thirties?

Add to that Gwen's ineradicable ghost-habits of poverty, her current shapeless guilt at being rich, at having a son who was not only off to college, but off to a college that cared not a tenth of a damn about "career development", or its graduate's post-graduation job or earning potential. Filthy lucre, n'est-ce pas? You can't excise the Jew from the Jewess.

From which genome did this bunny come? Like Will, Charles and Gwen lived through '67-'68, in a fortress similar to his, beyond the exploitation of man by man.

THE GREAT BATTLE (MAY DAY '68)

The landscape had changed from brown to green, while Will's general mood and outlook had marched counterclockwise.

Two things need to be cleared up:

1. How June became Will's Nausicaa and partner-in-crime

2. How May Day became the perfect day to start a war.

Concerning the first: the ice was easily broken: on the way home, heading back from his admissions interview, we recall Will chatting with June (it was *she*!) at her job at Earl's Sunoco. That was easy: she spoke first — "What can I do for you?"

A potentially dangerous question, but not at this time, at this place. There followed a memorized array of services to be offered to someone heading long-distance to New York, as his plates had indicated. The next move was somewhat trickier.

"How do you know so much about the Academy? Boyfriend?"

This was a stunning escalation, especially for Will, who was startled he had asked. But that that itinerary had been begun, and given her *she*-ness, continuing straight ahead was inevitable, even if at low velocity.

Her family, her dad the Admiral, "See you — not if I see you first", yada yada.

Then the letters over the summer. She had never received letters before. What midshipman would dare write letters to the young daughter of the Admiral Dean of Studies?

And that the Sunoco station was the drop? Earl was excited and proud — as if he were part of a CIA plot, in the role of Friar Lt. Lawrence. Nothing could happen to him: the post office would drop mail as it was addressed, and who would know about it except he who received the mail toward the end of the day, and the recipient, who was the only mail-getter in the box marked "employee mail". It was a closed system, though once received, the letters had

to be invisible in her home. Which they were, as she
never took them home, but memorized them, and
as early and repeatedly instructed within, dripping
with literary drama, (DESTROY THIS LETTER),
she most certainly did, burying them, all greased-up,
deep in the garbage barrel.

In Annapolis, there are no physical fences around St.
John's, and no walls around the Naval Academy. Yet
the psychic partitioning was as high as one might
imagine, and had continually enticed young June to
peek over.

Earl had agreed to employ her right out of the
nest, as it were, given an understanding with the
Admiral, her father, that Earl would protect her, and
toughen her up in his greasy world, an unpaid tutor.
Thus was his role even more conspiratorial, being a
double agent, playing both protector and procurer, all
for the delight of a private filling station drama.

June, once the emblematic gates were opened,
would devour the once-forbidden contents with
delight, a student whose perfection Will hadn't even

imagined. (He hadn't imagined having students, only
an audience for his antics. If he imagined sex at all,
it would have been with some studious, introverted
St. Johnnie with heavy green bookbag, and thick
eyeglasses.) He hadn't imagined having sex — and
with a high-level foreigner yet, but there it was: his
first, and hers.

As for June, the little devil enjoyed being
mischievous as she could be, playing out many
previously forbidden roles, including that of forbidden
fruit, and high-calorie dessert.

He shared his *Odyssey* with her, then bought her
own copy. She zeroed in on Nausicaa, "the burner
of ships", though she rejected his calling her that,
no matter how many "a"s there were. Besides, she
certainly wasn't shy.

Rejecting many of his assignments, she created
her own curriculum, paralleling his. For Sophocles'
Antigone, she substituted Anouilh's. For Aristophanes
Clouds, she substituted Joyce's sexier *Ulysses* (never
finished), for *Oedipus Rex*, she substituted *Ubu Roi*,
and for Thucydides *Peloponnesian War*, she read *War*

of the Worlds. They converged again on Euripides' *Bacchae*, though she had purchased a bilingual copy as she planned to start studying Greek.

You can imagine that her attendance at St. John's events (previously reported), in all her costumed glory, flowed easily from her frolicking participation in the Great Books Curriculum.

How May Day became the day of the Great Battle contained more complex questions: Which May Day? Which day of the Great Battle? Which Great Battle?

To simplify, let's just say that the first Annapolis May Day featured the great Battle of the Bands, and the second didn't.

Wednesday, May 1st, 1968, 47° (it would hit 70° at 6PM), clear, cloudless skies.

At 8AM, or rather 0800 hours, precisely, the St. John's campus was awakened by the approaching strains of *Anchors Away*. The Naval Academy Band was marching down College Ave., heading for and entering through the College's main gate to challenge the school at large to a duel. Leading the march, by virtue of his Hearndon Climb status, and his now-well-known role as cuckold, was once-Midshipman North of Texas, cornettist no longer, now a drum major, whose mace was an AR-15 with bayonet fixed.

And behind the band was a company of artillery, rifles strapped on shoulders, and who knew what was loaded in them? The band's fortissimo, and extra-accented sforzandos did not bode well, especially at this hour of the morning on a day historically linked, but vaguely associated with violence.

The response of the Johnnies to this unexpected attack? Not much, given that they were all getting ready for their nine o'clock classes.

One group of three, having rehearsed all the previous evening for a discussion/performance of the Brahms B major piano trio, had a unique, if experimental, thought.

The marching band was blaring their Sousa in D major. What if they pushed the piano out on the front porch, and dug into the B major Brahms.

The uninitiated reader may not know that the key of B major comes with five sharps.

Just the look of the key signature can be frightening, all those sharps flying at you like *hira shuriken*, throwing stars, slung by ninja masters.

Furthermore, the key of B major is like an alien invader in the world of D major. There is a natural relationship between D major and B *minor*. The B minor Mass is full of D major sections. But change that core D to D#, and it's like putting a cat's head onto a chicken. The most unflinching of us would flee before it. As well they should.

So, the Johnnie trio thought, striking up a fierce B major movement, the first of the Brahms they had been rehearsing for a month, might very well scare the D-majorists away, collapse their security, stick a pin into their balloon. They could really play the hell out of that piece!

However:

First, three instruments, even a piano plus two strings, can never overcome a marching band of twenty-five — even attacking their D major with B major. It's unlikely that the marchers even noticed the effort. They certainly didn't hear it over their own din.

Second, the Naval Academy Marching Band had a job to do — to scare the shit out of St. John's and the Johnnies, and to warn of, or at least to announce, a coming attack. En guard! It's only fair. Midshipmen do not shirk.

Enough musicology.

Let us now distinguish two different May Day-ish events or traditions:

First, we have a centuries-long European party day, a Rite of Spring long before Stravinsky, wine-fueled dancing around a ribboned maypole. Though via Hawthorne, we learn of the Puritan's war against the maypole and its dancers, their dark theology never prevailed against the lengthening of the days.

In 1885, the American Federation of Labor passed a resolution calling for an 8-hour working day, to go into effect on May 1st of the following year. The resolution was backed up by the threat of a general strike, should the call for shorter hours be denied. That was May Day #1 — violence theoretical, but potentially real.

And real it did become. On May 3 of the following year, workers at the McCormack Reaper Works in Chicago, on promised strike for an 8-hour day, were assaulted by company goons and the Chicago police, and several workers were wounded or killed.

A mass demonstration at Haymarket Square was called the next day, May 4, to protest the previous day's police violence. Radical and Anarchist speakers riled up a crowd of 1,500. When the police tried to disperse the peaceful crowd, the mood changed. Someone threw a bomb high in the air, its shrapnel wounding many. The police fired into the panicked crowd for two full minutes. Seven police and four civilians were killed, and more than a hundred injured.

The riot was blamed on the labor movement, and amidst public hysteria, seven people were tried and sentenced to death. May fourth became the second "May Day".

Law Day, Loyalty Day

So here we were on Wednesday, May 1st, 1968, which, by the way, was officially Law Day, or Loyalty Day, depending on which starboard direction you chose to survey. In 1958 President Eisenhower had declared May 1 to be "Law Day" in the United States to celebrate the rule of law, a declaration to reduce the portside influence of May Day, recently better known as International Workers' Day. It didn't work.

For example, in Annapolis, Maryland, there was lethal weaponry headed into the St. John's College booky campus. Law Day aside, which May Day was on the agenda — May first or May fourth? Neither seemed ideal.

Nevertheless, all went well. The challenge plan seemed to be symbolic, with the band marching into, and around campus, frontally serenading each inhabited building, and exiting as they had entered, out the front entrance, and back up College St. back into the Academy grounds they had left an hour earlier.

Though worrisome, the whole affair seemed to have been planned by the Grand Old Duke of York, or some current embodiment, the one who

had ten thousand men.
He marched the up to the top of the hill,
And marched them down again.

Perhaps it was just a playful variant for the morning's scheduled PT, though the fixed bayonets signaled rather more than the lyrics had noted:

And when they were up, the were up,
And when they were down, they were down,
And when they were only half-way up,
They were neither up nor down.

For by the time they were half-way around
the campus, the entire community was somewhere
between radically confused, and totally freaked-out.
This was 1968, Martin Luther King had just been
assassinated, the Soviet Union had just invaded
Czechoslovakia, and now the Navy was parading
around campus, early in the morning, triple-loud,
backed by fixed bayonets. Where was the Easter
Bunny when you needed him?

But that was only the first of the May Days,
neither up nor down. Nevertheless, Will was just as
happy June was not there to see it.

The second May Day, Saturday, May 4, 1968, had
begun the same way, another gorgeous morning im
wunderschönen Monat Mai. This is what it sounded
like at 8AM on the green, sheltered campus:

https://tinyurl.com/234zaexy

The buds were budding, and the birds, in
fact, were singing, and many a Johnnie heart was

longing to see some particular someone in class that day.

But it was not what it sounded like a 0800 hours. For those who lived in that time frame, it sounded more like *Anchors Aweigh* again, the *Navy Fight Song*, the only song the whole band could play without music — and as if they meant it.

Every fourth repeat, they broke out in chorus:

Stand, Navy, out to sea, Fight our battle cry;
We'll never change our course, So vicious foe steer shy-y-
y-y.
Roll out the TNT, Anchors Aweigh. Sail on to
victory
And sink their bones to Davy Jones, hooray!

The Johnnies were hardly vicious foes, and one midshipman wordsmith suggested "so *wimpy schmoes* steer shy-y-y-y", but he was outvoted by a large majority who preferred to stick with military tradition.

Davy Jones, however, was quite close by, just a few blocks southeast — the Severn River leading to

Chesapeake Bay, and south, around to the Atlantic. So they didn't argue about that. In fact, they kind of liked it.

What they, however, did not realize was that the campus was no longer the one they had bullied three days earlier. The Johnnies of high IQ had realized that this was serious business, and that something had to be done to protect the community from future raids. So on the day after the initial assault, they undertook a cleansing of the campus.

First, of course, they had gathered, tutti, for the largest mass singing of Palestrina's *Sicut Cervus* that had ever occurred — probably anywhere. The three-minute choral piece had somehow, somewhere, become the unofficial school song. What other college has a religious motet for its fight song?

> *Sicut cervus desiderat ad fontes aquarum,*
> *ita desiderat anima mea ad te, Deus.*

> *As a hart longs for the flowing streams,*
> *so longs my soul for thee, O God.*

Shades of Bambi!

98% of these kids knew nothing of Biblical psalms before coming to SJC. They probably knew nothing of Bambi. The only souls they knew, even then, belonged to ancient Greeks or Egyptians, not one another. And God was a non-starter. They were into "the gods".

Nevertheless, *Sicut Cervus* had become a long tradition, a semi-reflex group response to any threatening cloud. They sang it slowly, with eyes closed, all smelling of Dr. Bronners', swaying together back and forth like blades of grass with hairy seed pods up top, standing religiously around a pendulum swaying in the pendulum pit. This was not some campy take-off on Edgar Allen Poe, but a genuine Foucault pendulum, four stories high, demonstrating the rotation of the earth to any who might not believe it. And theirs was not some off-hand presence, but, to quote one starry-eyed sophomore, "a real participation in the universe."

The air being cleared by planetary motion, it was time for long tones on the school bagpipe and didgeridoo from the World Music closet. In every class, there seemed to be Johnnies that thought it would be cool to learn to sound them. A little went a long way, and it was soon enough time to gather any weapons of defense. They may have been slight and few, but they were classic, used by warriors throughout the eons.

Out came the dozen weapons from fencing class, a collection of foils, épées and sabers used by romantic-looking young men and women, should fencing be their elected PT activity. They were, the Johnnies thought, surely the equal of any new-fangled gadget with many moving parts and predictable breakdown the Navy was likely to procure.

Out, too came the boats from the Boat Club, prepared for evacuation, via the Severn River if necessary. Even the croquet balls were neatly stacked for possible cannon fire, though a cannon had yet to be procured. Leonardo drawings were consulted.

Later Thursday afternoon, and all that evening, the school orchestra, wildly understaffed, brought out parts to the *1812 Overture*. They had no guns of course, and thought it uncouth to use recorded sound, so during the culmination, the defeat of the Marseillaise, the string players and percussionists yelled "bang" and "boom", and stamped their feet.

After dinner, the school chorus attempted a choral version of Messiah's "Thou shall break them", a tune and text known to many from the potter's shed, for use whenever they ritually smashed any faulty creations, easy enough to sing alone, spit gathering at the corners of the lips, but deucedly hard to sing fiercely together. By eleven, they were set. Locked and loaded.

But where was June?

On Friday, the two mascot axolotls were brought from their lab to the lobby of McDowell Hall. Just how they were to be deployed was still unclear, but their official student keeper thought it best to only gradually bring them into play.

You probably don't know as much about axolotls as you should, so here you go:

https://www.treehugger.com/things-you-dont-know-about-axolotl-4863490

You likely still wouldn't choose one as your school mascot, but consider:

— they look like unfinished children for their entire lives, a trait not uncommon among Johnnies moved to study mainly classics. Cute, if somewhat awful.

— they are quite rare, in axolotl form, native to one small area in Mexico, in student form, native only to SJC, though occasionally scattered elsewhere. The ones who don't get asked to dances.

— they eat a surprising amount of meat — hot dogs and deli sandwiches, and the like. One would think they would be mincing Bunthornes with a passion only for green vegetables, but one would be wrong. There was meat available three times a day in the stately dining hall, and they knocked those meals down. Must have been all that struggle between the Persians and the Greeks.

— they are mostly whitish, but often enough yellow or brown. And this was before equal opportunity became an enforced norm. It might have something to do with parents' ability to pay full freight.

— alas, they can't regenerate body parts, though that has yet to be actually tried in the lab.

So there they were, two axolotls in two 55 gallon tanks, in the entrance hall of the St. John's administration building, consciously cavorting for their viewers. That should do something.

Friday was largely quiet. Small bottles of skatol —

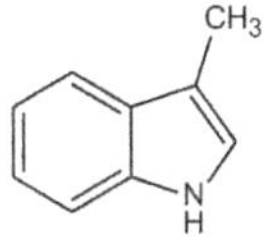

— the pretty little molecule that makes shit smell like shit — were, with some olfactory difficulty, prepared by stuffy-nosed geeks in chem lab according to instructions in the *Anarchist Cookbook.*

The NH does not stand for New Hampshire — the stuff stinks anywhere. The Navy needed no such cookery.

As far away from the lab as possible, fencing team students brought masks and protective vests back to their rooms with them. At the gym, the little-used medicine ball was noted as a possible band-stopper.

Will thought he'd better tank up the Green Hornet just in case.

Earl was in the office, but came out to the pump.

"Willy! Nice to see you. I hear there's all kinds of what goin' on over at the College."

"Season's Greetings, Earl. Seen June? I thought she'd be here."

"Hasn't been around for a couple of days. Wednesday afternoon some guys from the Yard came around to pick her up."

"Like officially? Was it a Navy car?"

"No, just some old brown Chevy. Three guys. Yardies. You know, polite. 'Sir' and all that. Seemed she knowed them."

"And she didn't come in to work yesterday or today?"

"Called in sick for a couple days. Sounded real hoarse on the phone. Me and the missus have been goin' it alone. Got any time to help out tomorrow — say just at the register?"

Oh, man! Not what Will needed. He drove off without buying any gas. Didn't really need it anyway.

By dinnertime, after dinner, by evening, June had not shown up.

At night, there were bongo drums and banjos, and a didgeridoo.

"The natives are restless," thought the men in white.

Friday night, Will had a most un-Will-like dream, disturbing in a curious way. While it had started — as one might imagine, given the threatening milieu — with an ape atop a gravestone, howling

in the sweet spring air, that ape sprang off, leaped
and scrambled over almost the entire contents
of Mahler's would-be death-postponement
attempt — loneliness, beautiful young girls, heroes
on horseback, late chats with friends, goodbyes
to childhood, parents, even a nod to the great
Whatever — skipped through all that and landed
— in spite of? because of? the day to come — on
what Will considered the only true miracle he had
ever attended, and could attend again and again
— the unthinkable, unimaginable, impossible key
changes toward the end of *der Abschied*, that huge
last song of the *Song of the Earth*. The "beloved earth
breaks into bloom each spring" — and on the word
"spring" the music transforms itself as if by magic,
the incomprehensible, hidden, total transformation
of pupa into butterfly within a tiny space, and
modulates, out of nowhere, from a simple C major, to
an unearthly Db major, and thence via unanalyzable
key gestures and colors, far out-Tristaning Tristan
on the word-notion of "everywhere" (the "all overall"
in German) to settle on the word "ewig", forever.

Ewig, ewig, ewig...repeated who knows how many times, "dying away" Mahler instructs, ending, pppp, pianoisisisimo, "altogether dying"... the last iteration ending on an unresolved D floating above C major. That most elaborate earworm occupied Will, pupa in his chrysalis, all through the night.

He woke up to Saturday morning, the second May Day. His S was for Odysseus, and his throat was sore. Had he been the howling ape?

The Navy band had prepared the Hallelujah chorus, with a full weight of extra beginner trombones entering at "for the Lord God Omnipotent reigneth", the Handel being their newly discovered fight song — for which they still needed to read the music.

The Academy Band's march through the main entrance, as before, was merely a clever military feint, for in the early morning hours, the cadets had stealthily stored their tools in the parking lot behind Iglehart Gym, and serially deployed them according to plan.

The opening Battle of the Bands didn't seem didn't seem more serious than Wednesday's. There were some great Charles Ives moments if you were standing in the right spot to hear them, and the Johnnies had added "Thou shalt smash them" to their armamentarium, and shouted victory passages from the *Iliad* — some of those same texts the midshipmen might have loved. They didn't come to much in the face of five trombones, three baritone horns, three euphoniums, and two tubas — a class war gesture at best. En guard? Allez!

But when the first shot rang out…O.'s first shot, or signal…when the first shot rang out, the genre of the event quickly changed. It was game or sport no more. Behind Saturday's band was not an orderly rank and file of shouldered (if bayoneted) rifles, but a serial display, in caliber order, of the armaments in the US Naval Museum.

That first shot broke a window in McDowell Hall, but hell, there were only administrators there. More serious was the second shot, into Campbell dorm, though most of the students were out already, at their posts assigned.

The third shot was the most serious, even though only into Randall Dining Hall. It may have been a bullet, or may itself have been an incendiary, but a fire broke out and spread quickly.

An earlier Johnnie alumnus, Francis Scott Key, might have scribbled on his Homer something like

O thus be it ever when freemen shall stand
Between their lov'd home and the war's desolation!

though it wouldn't be clear which freemen he'd now be cheering on. The current female students carried pots of water from the kitchen to try to extinguish the blaze, while many of the males saw this as their chance to pull out their peepees and piss on the fire, since in their chemistry courses, they learn that male urine is sterile, and even drinkable in extremis. It would certainly be a righteous tool with which to save their alma mater.

There entered from various directions a two-wheeled artillery cannon, a small self-propelled field howitzer, and four light mortars — in which shells were dropped onto a fixed firing pin. As with everything Navy, all had been kept in tip-top shape, cleaned and oiled for maximal lethality. The platoon fired at various buildings according to an ordinance plan made by someone who knew the Johnnie campus well, its patterns and traffic flow, maximizing the spread of fire, and also the safety of its human inhabitants — though collateral damage they might become — as the goal was to reduce the campus and all its books to rubble and ashes. The and the basement bookstore in Humphreys were key, the Great Books being not only hot, but quite flammable targets.

It was the appearance of the amphibious assault vehicle track personnel carrier that prompted Will to run for the Green Hornet, now, as always, parked behind the admissions building, an unpunished transgression that had persisted so long as to appear normal. Perhaps it was the president's car in the president's parking space at the admission to the pearly gates? Who knew? Why should anyone inquire? But would President Weigle drive a '51 Hudson Hornet? A green one?

Do you know what an amphibious assault vehicle is? It is 26 feet long, 11 feet wide, 11 feet high, and empty of personnel, weighs 32 tons. That's 64,000 pounds. Empty. Then add the fuel, the three operators, and the thirty or so Trojan Warriors poised impatiently inside, weapons at the ready, gas masks in their packs, and chewing gum and spare change in their pockets. That's heavy.

Trojan Warriors? The Trojan Horse would be chartreuse with envy. Traveling on tank treads at up to 20mph, armed with a grenade launcher, and two heavy machine guns, it was more than a match for eighteenth century wooden buildings faced in red brick. It had been cooped up too long in its stall in the yard, and was newly polished, pawing the ground and rarin' to go. No picadors needed. It did not belong on the green lawns and thin walkways of St. John's College.

If one such monster invaded your living space, wouldn't you react? Will did. He would even things out: internal combustion vs. internal combustion, horsepower vs. horsepower, gasoline vs. diesel, emerald green vs. navy drab, style vs. sting. He ran for the Green Hornet, drove it right up to a flaming McDowell Hall in the middle of the quad, and jumped out, ticket or no ticket, parked in the most prohibited parking space imaginable. Up roared the carrier from his rear, and unloaded its cargo of thirty troops. At their head, leading them into the fray, was...June, surrounded by a personal guard of six — though whether the rifles were meant to protect her or keep her from running away wasn't clear.

To tell the truth, she didn't look all that happy, dolled up as — was it Lady Liberty? Please..no! Her costume was that of Delacroix's *Liberty Leading the People*: tan dress with white underblouse, more modestly worn, but fierce nonetheless, barefooted, bayoneted rifle in left hand, and right hand raising high the blue banner of the US Naval Academy, with its two torches aflame, its trident labeled "SCIENTIA" and its shield bearing boat, book, and waves.

In fact, her hair wrapped in a Phrygian Bonnet, her cheeks reddened with — what? —passion? anger? having been too long inside a troop carrier? —June looked a little tarted up, something her admiral Daddy might be embarrassed by.

But hmm — her Admiral Daddy, Dean of Academic Studies. How would these sailorly lunkheads, with their close-cropped heads and shiny boots, how would *they* have known about the two May Days, how would *they* have been able to distinguish between them so carefully, and plan so strategically? And who could have costumed June with such scholarly — if fatherly — precision? Why, all along, had she been so promiscuous, and Daddy so permissive?

The light dawned at last, the plot thickened. It all fell into place, aha!, the Great Treason, the classical Mata Hari routine, probably taught at the Academy to harden its students against perilous onshore events. Yes, Will thought, it had been planned all along, and probably by Daddy, dean of monsterly Studies, the final excuse for a long-desired military invasion of Western civilization! The old Montague-Capulet routine, a classic. Find the hydrophilic boy and the hydrophobic girl, rub them up against one another, front to front, and, boom!, the structure self-destructs.

Will, a prop no longer, but bursting with agency, jumped into the Hornet, and backed fiercely up, forgetting that the troop carrier was three feet behind him, piling into its hardened front bumper, crushing the empty rear of the Hudson, and almost bringing down a sailor who had wandered between them. The carrier pilot, with limited vision and primitive patriotism, decided to punish the attacker, applying the Law of the Most Massive he'd learned in class, and pushed quickly and hard against the wounded Hornet, smashing its front into the McDowell steps, green and chrome on red. F = ma, and m was huge. Will was in-between. And where was June?

It was barely 9AM. The police and ambulance took only minutes to arrive, and the once-Will, extracted with the Jaws of Life, was carted off to Anne Arundel Medical Center, and there pronounced DOA. A death of the firstborn.

Earl towed the crumpled Hudson to the closest auto graveyard, where they paid out ten bucks, which would likely exceed what was salvageable in parts. Daddy took June back to her home at the Academy, where she spent the next two years under taxpayer-provided, closely supervised psychiatric care.

Old St. Earl, in high Friar Lawrence mode, felt moved and responsible enough to drive the transit casket all the way to Mount Kisco in his auto hauler, showing appropriate papers at each state line and toll stop.

At late-afternoon cocktails, Charles and Gwen wondered why a tow truck would be pulling up in front of their house. The Rolls, the Mercedes, and

the Packard, were sleeping peacefully in their stalls,
equally uninformed.

Earl, his papers, and his load, were directed by
the now-appalled, half-hysterical parents — after
consulting the Yellow Pages — to the closest
mortuary, a destination never before researched
— Dignity Funeral Home & Services. There,
the cardboard casket was carefully unloaded and
carried with dignity to the preparation room up the
driveway in the rear.

Though about to leave for the day, when the
container arrived, Randy, Jim, and Lamont went
off resignedly to the locker room to change back
into work clothes and gloves, transferred the casket
onto a work table — and took a coffee break before
beginning their disinfecting, draining of blood and
filling with embalming fluid, dressing, and removal to
the elegant, tastefully-carved wooden coffin chosen by
the Vanderbilt-Davidoffs, fully prepared for viewing.

Returning from break, they found the casket
open.

An FBI APB was put out for New York and surrounding states, and William Eugene Vanderbilt-Davidoff was charged with kidnapping, interstate flight, obstruction of justice, suicide, and murder in the first degree.

The case remains unsolved, but, like the coffin, open.

About the Author

Marc Estrin is a writer and editor in Burlington Vermont.

Fomite

Writing a review on social media sites for readers will help the progress of independent publishing. To submit a review, go to the book page on any of the sites and follow the links for reviews. Books from independent presses rely on reader-to-reader communications.

For more information or to order any of our books, visit:
http://www.fomitepress.com/our-books.html

More novels and novellas from Fomite...

Joshua Amses — *During This, Our Nadir*
Joshua Amses — *Ghats*
Joshua Amses — *Raven or Crow*
Joshua Amses — *The Moment Before an Injury*
Charles Bell — *The Married Land*
Charles Bell — *The Half Gods*
Jaysinh Birjepatel — *Nothing Beside Remains*
Jaysinh Birjepatel — *The Good Muslim of Jackson Heights*
David Brizer — *The Secret Doctrine of V. H. Rand*
David Brizer — *Victor Rand*
L. M Brown — *Hinterland*
Paula Closson Buck — *Summer on the Cold War Planet*
L.enny Cavallaro — *Paganini Agitato*
Dan Chodorkoff — *Loisaida*
Dan Chodorkoff — *Sugaring Down*
David Adams Cleveland — *Time's Betrayal*
Paul Cody — *Sphyxia*
Jaimee Wriston Colbert — *Vanishing Acts*

Fomite

Roger Coleman — *Skywreck Afternoons*
Stephen Downes — *The Hands of Pianists*
Marc Estrin — *Hyde*
Marc Estrin — *Kafka's Roach*
Marc Estrin — *Proceedings of the Hebrew Free Burial Society*
Marc Estrin — *Speckled Vanities*
Marc Estrin — *The Annotated Nose*
Marc Estrin — *The Penseés of Alan Krieger*
Zdravka Evtimova — *Asylum for Men and Dogs*
Zdravka Evtimova — *In the Town of Joy and Peace*
Zdravka Evtimova — *Sinfonia Bulgarica*
Zdravka Evtimova — *You Can Smile on Wednesdays*
Daniel Forbes — *Derail This Train Wreck*
Peter Fortunato — *Carnevale*
Greg Guma — *Dons of Time*
Ramsey Hanhan – *Fugitive Dreams*
Richard Hawley — *The Three Lives of Jonathan Force*
Lamar Herrin — *Father Figure*
Michael Horner — *Damage Control*
Ron Jacobs — *All the Sinners Saints*
Ron Jacobs — *Short Order Frame Up*
Ron Jacobs — *The Co-conspirator's Tale*
Scott Archer Jones — *A Rising Tide of People Swept Away*
Scott Archer Jones — *And Throw Away the Skins*
Julie Justicz — *Conch Pearl*
Julie Justicz — *Degrees of Difficulty*
Maggie Kast — *A Free Unsullied Land*
Darrell Kastin — *Shadowboxing with Bukowski*
Coleen Kearon — *#triggerwarning*

Fomite

Coleen Kearon — *Feminist on Fire*
Jan English Leary — *Thicker Than Blood*
Jan English Leary — *Town and Gown*
Diane Lefer — *Confessions of a Carnivore*
Diane Lefer — *Out of Place*
Rob Lenihan — *Born Speaking Lies*
Cynthia Newberry Martin — *The Art of Her Life*
Colin McGinnis — *Roadman*
Douglas W. Milliken — *Our Shadows' Voice*
Ilan Mochari — *Zinsky the Obscure*
Peter Nash — *In the Place Where We Thought We Stood*
Peter Nash — *Parsimony*
Peter Nash — *The Least of It*
Peter Nash — *The Perfection of Things*
George Ovitt — Stillpoint
George Ovitt — Tribunal
Gregory Papadoyiannis — *The Baby Jazz*
Pelham — *The Walking Poor*
Christopher Peterson — *Madman*
Andy Potok — *My Father's Keeper*
Frederick Ramey — *Comes A Time*
Howard Rappaport — *Arnold and Igor*
Joseph Rathgeber — *Mixedbloods*
Kathryn Roberts — *Companion Plants*
Robert Rosenberg — *Isles of the Blind*
Fred Russell — *Rafi's World*
Ron Savage — *Voyeur in Tangier*
David Schein — *The Adoption*
Charles Simpson — *Uncertain Harvest*

Fomite

* 9 7 8 1 9 5 9 9 9 8 4 4 0 5 *